D1595746

S.C. 813.54 GODW c.3

Godwin, Rebecca T.

Private Parts

S.C. 813.54 GODW c.3

Godwin, Rebecca T.

Private Parts

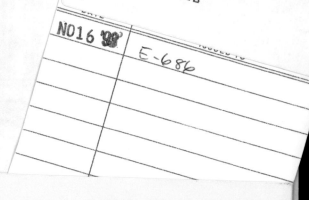

NO16 '93

E-686

South Carolina State Library
Columbia, S.C.

GAYLORD

DATE

PRIVATE
PARTS

REBECCA T. GODWIN

LONGSTREET PRESS
Atlanta, Georgia

Published by
LONGSTREET PRESS, INC.
2140 Newmarket Parkway
Suite 118
Marietta, Georgia 30067

Copyright © 1991 by Rebecca T. Godwin

All rights reserved. No part of this book may be reproduced
in any form or by any means without the prior written
permission of the Publisher, excepting brief quotes used in
connection with reviews, written specifically for inclusion in a
magazine or newspaper.

Printed in the United States of America

1st printing 1992

ISBN: 1-56352-021-4

Library of Congress Catalog Number: 91-77186

This book was printed by R. R. Donnelley & Sons,
Harrisonburg, Virginia. The text was set in Optima by Typo-
Repro Service, Inc., Atlanta, Georgia.

Jacket design and illustration by Shelley Lowell

The following chapters first appeared in other publications:
"Moving On" (as "Thomas") in *Iris, A Journal about Women;*
"Over Bridge" (as "Mac's Will") in *South Carolina Review;*
and "Seeds" in *The Crescent Review.*

All characters and events in this book are purely fictional. Any
resemblance to actual events or people, living or dead, is a
matter of coincidence.

*To my parents
in their 50th year together
with love*

Acknowledgments

I would like to thank everyone who encouraged and sustained me through the writing of this book, but must content myself with these few: my children and extended family, especially sisters; Tracy and David, Page and Pinky and Roy; Martha and Temp; Jane Hill; the folks at Longstreet; the Hills of Poestenkill; Lisa DiMona; pure grace; and my husband Deane Bogardus, who read the manuscript— mostly with good humor and always with a sharp eye—more times than anyone should ever have to.

Prologue

Lie flat and put one arm under your head.

I do that and feel like one of those old-timey pinup girls, Betty Grable maybe, else Jayne Mansfield. You know how they always put one arm under their heads, like they were abandoned women, wild and reckless.

Keep propping this magazine up to see the instructions, but it sags to one side and then closes every time. The pages fan my face. I anchor it against the husband on my bed. It's a corduroy-covered, dusty rose one, which I bought last month when I decorated this room.

They call it a husband, I reckon, because of the soft stuffed arms that reach around to circle you from behind. You can lean on it, all night if you want, all day too, and it'll support you without offering one word of backtalk. Doesn't snore, either.

Dusty rose and slate blue's what I did the room in. Jimmy Lee's favorite color is yellow. One of our guest rooms was done in it. Put my teeth on edge to go in there, felt like I was on the inside of a buttercup. Had to squint to see.

Can't help but be reminded right now how Jimmy Lee always loved my breasts, even when nothing else about me suited him. I am pondering that, or anything else, as I lie here trying to prop this magazine so I can follow the directions exactly and not think what it means to be doing this.

Prop a folded towel beneath your back for support.

I don't have one and I don't want to get up again, so I use part of the pillow. When we were first married, Jimmy Lee was always wanting to stick a pillow under me. Right in the middle of doing it, he'd reach over and get one and try to prop me up with it. I'd grab the thing and throw it off the bed. Sometimes we'd practically wrestle. Never did discuss it afterwards, so I don't know what he was thinking, but I was thinking about that pillowcase getting messy and having to replace it with one from the other set of sheets and then it'd have to be on there a whole week unmatched like that and by the time you went to the next set of sheets, that pillowcase'd be dirty, so you'd have to use the other one and nothing would ever match. He finally quit trying, which was likely a relief to us both.

The article says to do this once a month, right after your period. Says to mark the time by that. Right after your period, it says, your breasts are less lumpy than usual. Something to do with hormones. Doesn't say when to do it if you don't have a period anymore. Maybe they think women who don't have periods anymore don't need to do this. At least Margaret A. Swinton must think that. She wrote this article. I bet she's about twenty-four, kind of perky, with blonde hair and long legs.

Imagine the breast as a circle, she says. *Press two fingers down firmly and begin making a circular motion, working from the outside in.*

Now I don't know about you, but when I lie down like this and put my arm behind my head, most of my bosom slides sideways, to my underarm. From the directions, I can't tell if that's supposed to be part of the circle or not, but I can't imagine a circle that goes way off to the side like that, it'd be more like an oval or an oblong, so I guess not.

I remember walking in on my grandmomma one time. I must have been around six or seven. We were visiting her in North Carolina. She lived in a little tree-shaded house with a glassed-in porch and a backyard that had Spanish moss hanging off the oaks and a rope swing where I ate watermelon and watched ants haul the pink leftovers through the dirt to the next yard. Gramma had soft white hair fluffed out around a fallen-in face you had to love and an egg timer in her kitchen that she sometimes let me play with. One day I walked into her bedroom when she was getting dressed. She had a half-slip on. Her bare back was to me, the empty cups of her brassiere dangling waist-high. She was fastening it in front. When she heard me, she turned around, saying, "Oh, honey, you gave me a start."

Lord knows, it was mutual. I had seen Momma's bosoms—small, high points of rose-colored flesh—and once, in a magazine by Daddy's side of the bed, I had seen page after page of breasts like huge flesh balloons tacked onto bodies. But here were two pale, thin, *long* bosoms, hanging down beyond her waist, swaying gently as she turned.

In the face she was my grandmomma, but in the body, oh, in the body were these monstrous white worms with pale pink noses. She smiled, turned her brassiere around, scooped first one and then the other into the waiting cups, and hiked the whole thing up onto her shoulders where the straps slipped into deep, worn grooves.

I never looked at her again without thinking of what was hiding underneath her clothes. When she hugged me, sometimes I thought I'd scream. She died two years later, and I was sorry then for those short hugs.

That was my first leavetaking, Gramma's. It should have taught me about being sorry for things you can't do over, but I don't reckon it did.

I start under my arm anyway, just in case, and move my fingers firmly around. My flesh feels like someone else's. It is soft, cool to the touch. At the top of the first circle, one right next to the other, are two lumps. My breath comes ragged, like a caught sigh.

Do not be alarmed if you feel small lumps, Margaret tells me, and I can picture her perfect smile, see her shaking her head at my panic. *Lumps are normal. Breasts have irregular, fatty tissue.* I feel my other breast, in the same area. It has matching lumps. They must be the normal kind. I breathe and continue my circle.

I know bosoms're supposed to be sexy, but touching them like this doesn't make me feel sexy at all. Makes me feel kind of queasy instead, like when somebody cracks their knuckles and you hear things grinding inside.

I do this every month. Isn't that surprising? That I do this every month and still I have this magazine propped up, reading directions like a beginner? I need to do that, though, see? Takes my mind off the thing itself. Got a whole collection of how-to articles on self-examination—BSE, they call it. Switch them around every month so it doesn't get too tiresome, though I may let this Margaret A. Swinton one go after today.

Point is, I do this every month, and my breasts never feel the same twice. Lumps and knobs appear and disappear, nipples darken and lighten, skin tightens and loosens. Like trying to read a blueprint that keeps shifting under your fingers.

That's how it feels when I try to see my life, too. Means something different every time I look. And partly that scares me, and partly I like it. Surprises are always there, just below the surface, whether you're feeling around for them or not.

I read on ahead to the next part. *Take the nipple lightly between two fingers,* Margaret directs, *and if* she'd show her face right now, I might just slap it. *Squeeze gently, and check for any unusual discharge.* I don't do it yet, I just can't make myself, because for some reason, this is the part I hate most. I dread craning my head down to look, as though the moment I do, the truth will come flying out at me and I will be helpless before it.

Commencement

"Just tell me the truth, Mattie. It's all I ask."

Like that's not a lot.

Heard Bobby waiting, breathing into the phone, but couldn't get my mouth around an answer, why I don't know. Isn't like I wasn't expecting the question—been waiting on it all day, hearing it in my head like the echo of something hadn't sounded yet but had to, like the hum of telephone wires into the silence after his voice left off.

Which humming sound has been in my head ever since, even now, as I stand before the mirror in the hall bathroom of Mr. Jackson's house, fixing to go to my graduation, putting on a second coat of mascara and eying these creases in my bangs. I hate how Dippity-Do and tape'll do that. Wish my hair'd lie flat like Mary Lou Harter's. One edge is already pulling away from the rest, twisting itself up out of place.

Like me, I reckon, on account of I can't figure where my place is. Right now I don't seem to have one, considering the conversation me and Momma had last week.

"Can we talk a minute, Sister?" she says—long as I can remember Momma's called me that, why I don't know—but by how her eyes are hunting somewhere to rest besides on mine, I know something's up. She pulls out a chair at the kitchen table and sits down, holding her head between her two hands and not looking up at me. Ever since Daddy died, she's been wearing her hair back in a smooth bun. From where I'm standing, her neck looks skinny and pale, and I see the roots where her hair dye's wearing off.

Soon's I sit down, she brightens up, says, "Guess what, Sister?" And waits, like maybe I will. "We're moving to Mobile."

She tries a quick look up then, scanning my face. And something about the way she says *we* and the skittishness of her eyes makes it hard to look at her. I'm all of a sudden thinking about how things were for us before.

I carry a picture around in my head of my momma and daddy. Don't know how long it's been there because, to me, they always looked about the same age. My daddy was kind of skinny, even before he got sick. Tall, with bones you could almost see underneath his skin. Dark hair, thin, muscular legs. Momma's slim, too, with long, brown hair and eyes that turn up some at the corners. In my picture, they're in a kitchen, I can see the table behind them, and a counter. Momma has on shorts and a sleeve-less top and Daddy's wearing his work clothes, and they're dancing. The music isn't part of my picture, but there must be some because they're holding each other and looking into each other's eyes, swaying and sweeping to music I can't hear, and though I must be in the room, they don't know it. Momma laughs, I can tell by how she throws her head back, but I can't hear it—my picture's soundless as a dream—and when she does, Daddy kisses her neck and bends her backwards till it seems like she'd break with it, that bending.

But of course she didn't. He did, instead.

The other pictures in my head aren't soundless. They're full of the noise of his coughing, coughing, day-in-day-out coughing, till I could see Momma almost scream with it, standing in the kitchen alone, holding her shoulders in tight to keep from it.

Funny, how he was the one to get lung cancer. Never smoked a cigarette in his life, though it was practically a sin not to when you worked for R. J. Reynolds, which he'd done ever since he's a boy. Lot of people he worked with smoked three or four packs a day, just to prove their loyalty.

Momma, on the other hand, who did not get sick and die, smoked one cigarette after another, from her first cup of coffee in the morning till the lights went out in their room at night. Sometimes even after—I remember walking down the hall to the bathroom and looking in to see the red glow of her cigarette in their pitch black room. Not that Daddy minded,

3

wouldn't of minded if she'd set fires with it, or put cigarettes out in the palm of his hand. Whether she was smoking, talking, eating, or just blinking, his eyes'd follow her every move. Lovesick, long as I can remember, way before he got really sick. After, he'd wait like a starved dog for her to come stroke her hand across his forehead or murmur something sweet and soothing. And sometimes she would, but I remember her more often hunched over in the kitchen, listening to his cough.

Four months to the day after we buried Daddy, she married Mr. Jackson, with his three kids and this house, and his managerial position at A&P which's got him transferring to Mobile. Now Momma's trying to quit smoking because he says it isn't ladylike. She smokes in the bathroom sometimes, though, I've seen her, standing on the potty and blowing the smoke up through the ventilator. Quit her checker's job, too, because Mr. Jackson said it wasn't right, them both working there, and now she wears her hair up in this tight bun. We all go to church on Sunday. And hard as I try, I can't picture her ever again throwing her head back in a soundless laugh.

When I close my eyes tight right now and open them back up real fast to see can I catch myself by surprise, I look like Daddy. Something about my darkness and a turn of cheek. Else maybe through the eyes, a yearning. I like that, but in another second I've lost it, lost even the memory of exactly how he did look.

Pure, hot panic rises up inside me as I stand here before Mr. Jackson's mirror. In that little quickness of time, seem like things've always been like this— Momma with a bun and Daddy gone—and all the rest a dream, or somebody else's life.

That's how it seemed last week, too, sitting there looking at the top of Momma's head while she's inspecting her lap. I have the strongest urge to reach across the table and slap her hard as I know how, but instead I take a deep breath and say, "Well, maybe I won't go, Momma."

Then she tips her head up ever so slightly, and just before she closes her eyes, what I see in them is something that looks to me like relief. I say nothing and she says nothing, we just sit there, like maybe in a minute something's going to change. But it doesn't. And when I get tired of hearing myself swallow, I leave.

Daddy always used to tell me, "Don't think so much, girl. You're going to strain your brain." And I'm trying to take his advice, but it's not easy. Right now, for instance, I'm trying to think of nothing but putting just the right amount of Erase on this pimple in the smack center of my chin that swears it's going to graduation with me. You got to be careful. Put it on too thick and it looks gooey, calls attention worse than the thing you're trying to cover up.

Like that humming noise that's stayed in my head ever since yesterday. Hard as I try, I can't cover it up. Can't pretend that not telling Bobby anything at all isn't the same as flat out lying. And can't explain myself to myself well enough to see how come I did what I did.

First time I saw Bobby McAllister—it was after school, at Whistler's Drive-in; September, and Daddy dead less than a month—I thought to myself that he was different from the other boys in Red Hill. Not that I knew a lot about them, hadn't been here but a year. Wasn't just his car either, though I will say it caught my eye, a two-tone, aqua-colored '56 Chevy he keeps so nice it looks brand new. There was just something about his eyes, watching as I walked up to the car—soft, brown eyes, gentle, not looking nasty and chest-high, how some of the older boys do, or sniggling and punching each other, like the high-school ones. He was just friendly looking and polite, which is unusual enough, around here. So by the third time I waited on him and he asked would I go to the show with him that Friday night, I didn't change words, except to say yes.

Wasn't much of anybody to tell about it. At school, I tend to keep to myself. Red Hill's mostly people who been here since time began, or before. Everybody's kin to everybody else, and somebody who's spent her life moving from one little place to the next doesn't fit with girls who remember each other's first word, first tooth, first Barbie doll. Not to mention the clothes situation—they buy theirs down at Turner's on Front Street, else from Charleston, whereas Sears Roebuck is not a word in their vocabulary.

Can't say they go out of their way to be snobby, though. It's more like I don't exist on the same planet.

And I don't think having big bosoms helps, either, which I always did. Get them from Daddy's side of the family, according to Momma. And from the time they started pushing through, they hadn't much slowed down, which to tell the truth is something I could do without—boys tend to act fool over them, and girls whisper and cut their eyes sideways when we change after gym class.

Anyhow, wasn't a soul to talk to. Momma was working long hours down at the A&P. Already seeing Mr. Jackson more than likely, though not letting on to me. Whenever I told her I was going out with somebody I met at Whistler's, she gave me that look of hers that stops short of seeing me, and said, "Just be careful, Sister." Whatever that means.

Well, I reckon I do know what it means. Not that she ever went into much detail or said anything more direct than commenting how nice girls keep themselves pure for their husbands. Pure. "I was pure as the driven snow, Sister, the day your Daddy and I got married."

Hadn't ever had a problem staying that way up to now myself, what with us moving all the time and Daddy's getting sick. But Bobby changed that.

First it was the kisses, in the front seat of his car, at the drive-in movie on Fountain Road—some on my lips and some on my ears and my neck and then back to my lips again—soft, sweet kisses that go on and on till my breath comes short. Something goes warm inside, in the neighborhood of my belly, then spreads itself out all over, like a slow, sleepy hum, and

I feel like nothing so much as just letting go, opening my arms and my legs and my lips, letting Bobby in. Turning myself inside out for him. Lord.

Sometimes we get in the back seat of his Chevy, where he presses himself full-length against me and sometimes brushes his lips, barely touching, against the tip ends of my breasts. Just through the clothes — never unhooks my bra — which I want him to so bad I could scream with it.

But Bobby says when you're in love, you got to wait. His whole body shakes with the waiting, and by the time I get home, my nipples are so tight they ache. I lie on my bed and press them down into it. Sometimes, I touch myself where memory still feels the hardness of Bobby through his jeans and my skirt. Touch myself, pretending it's him, till that slow hum changes to a rising-up feeling that turns my heart to an engine I can hear the roar of inside my ears. And I find myself thinking about that, and about Bobby, till it's hard to think about anything else.

Seem to me that kind of feeling is what drove my daddy, a hungering like this for Momma, a hungering that couldn't get filled up, that never went away, humming in his head day and night till it finally moved down, desperation filling his lungs and choking him.

Sometimes, when I'm staring at Bobby, filling my head with the look of his face or an angle of wrist-bone in a certain light, I get scared. Somewhere deep inside I feel like I might could turn into my daddy, like if I looked in a mirror at just that instant, I'd see him instead of me. The fear comes up in my throat till I turn my head away and make my mind smooth and blank.

Bobby works at the paper mill over in Lawton, the county seat, fifteen miles from here—same as about half the people in Red Hill. When the wind's right, the smell from that mill gets into your car, your clothes, your hair—right up into your skin. Hard to get rid of. Around here they say it's the smell of bread and butter, and you can tell they been saying that same thing for a hundred years, or however long IP's been around. Anyhow, Bobby works shift work there, just like his daddy. Says he won't always do it, though. Wants to go to college one day, make something of himself. Just you wait, he says.

And maybe that's it, I don't know. Maybe I can't see it, waiting. Been waiting seventeen years for my life to take a turn. So then whenever it's offered me, why shouldn't I say yes?

Anyhow, I was too surprised not to, the way that boy popped up right in front of me last week—me walking down the hall, thinking about would Bobby call that night, and him planting himself right in front of me saying, hey, I've had my eye on you, what about you and me going to the show this weekend. And those other boys standing by their lockers, laughing low and looking sideways at us. Me, shocked, stuttering out a yes. Jimmy Lee Turner. I knew who he was, waited on him lots of times down at Whistler's. Anyhow, everybody knows who Jimmy Lee Turner is. By the end of the day, everybody knew who I was, because of him. It was like being picked for prom queen out the clear blue, when you didn't know you were running. Mary Lou Harter even walked beside me to French class, called me by name. Which I didn't even know she knew.

Even though Momma likes Bobby—you can tell by how she fusses with her hair and talks to him when he comes to pick me up, seems a little like her old self then—she didn't hesitate when I told her about Jimmy Lee. "Go after him, Sister," she said, "while you got the chance."

Here's the thing. Jimmy Lee's family's pretty big around Red Hill, between owning the best department store in town and being around long as anybody. Kin to the Hamiltons, too. Who were practically Pilgrims or something.

So when Bobby called that night, the subject of Jimmy Lee Turner did not come up. We just talked about this and that, nothing special. It's not like we ever promised anything out loud. I'm not even wearing his ring. And anyhow, he's working three to eleven on the weekend. Course that didn't matter, in terms of him finding out, small towns being how they are.

Momma came into the bathroom Friday night while I was getting ready, showed me how to use eye shadow to make my eyes look bigger. "Keep wetting your lips like this, Sister," she told me, demonstrating the technique. "Men don't care for dry-lipped women."

After graduation tonight I might see Jimmy Lee, he asked me where was I going, after. Although why he'd want to see me again after our date I don't know.

Last Friday when he picked me up, he asked where did I want to go and I said I didn't know, so we went to the drive-in. First thing he did was put his arm across the back of the seat. All during the show he kept scooting closer and closer. By intermission he was almost on my lap, me trying to be polite and getting up next to the door till the handle pressed my back. Hardly changed a half dozen words all evening, just silent moves in the front seat of his daddy's new Lincoln, gold with brown leather interior. Finally I said I needed a Coke and popcorn, which he went and got, which I commenced to eat slow as I knew how during the second half. And when Jimmy Lee kissed me good-night in front of my door, I know for a fact he got a mouthful of salt. So I find it surprising he's called me twice since Friday. But maybe I'm as big a puzzlement to him as he is to me. Or maybe it just comes down to bosoms, which is more likely.

That humming sound in my head is driving me plumb crazy, so when I go back into my room — the one I share with Tonya, Mr. Jackson's oldest, she's eight — I turn the radio up loud. Putting on my graduation dress — it's pure white, with a Peter Pan collar and a drop waist, Momma surprised me with it this morning, telling how it came from Turner's and wasn't even on sale — I try not to see myself in the little mirror over Tonya's dresser. Not that I think I'd look like Daddy today, just that I'd rather not know.

"Mattie," Bobby's voice didn't have anger in it, even though it could have, deserved to, maybe that would've made a difference.

"Is it true, were you with him?" Still I said nothing, could say nothing, the hum going on and on, me holding the phone like it was salvation I couldn't reach for, hearing his breathing over the hum and remembering the sweet feel of his breath on my neck.

"Momma," I call, and when I go out into the hall, I have this feeling of stepping into some other life altogether. "I'm ready."

Seem like lately I can't get my mouth around the truth to save my life.

Last Night

"Goddammit, Mat." His face was pinked up and he's panting a little, the edges of his hair wet from sweat. I was hot too, my legs sticking to the leather in the back seat of his daddy's car.

"Why not?" I could smell his sweat as he hung over me. "Just give me one good reason why not." Right that minute, Jimmy Lee Turner looked like nothing so much as a spoiled little boy, whining after some toy he's wanting and couldn't have.

I looked up at the ceiling of the car, which had little pinpricks all over it. Didn't open my mouth, no call to, been over this till he could spit it back to me word for word, if he'd a mind to. Don't reckon he did, though.

Should've said something, probably, because, as usual, he took silence for yes, and here came one sly hand out again, fingering the edge of my shorts, moving lightly in a circle on the skin of my thigh, like he thought maybe he could hypnotize me into not knowing what he's up to.

All's I did was sigh and move his hand over to his lap, where there wasn't any hiding how he felt. We'd been doing this same thing, or something like it, for going on three months.

That time, a kind of sob sounded in his throat, and I was thinking to myself, that's the last straw, probably, thinking: I'm not sorry, I'm not.

"That's it, then," he said, moving back from me, slumping against the seat, grabbing his hair with both hands like a person about to lose his mind. Looking up at the ceiling of the car, he heaved a big, tired sigh, and then said it, practically strangling on the words. "Let's just get married."

That was about a month ago, and yesterday I married Jimmy Lee Turner, and last night we finally had sex—twice—and this morning we're sharing a bed. Hope he thinks it was worth it.

Never been in a bed this big. It's a king-size one. He's way over there, snoring away, and I'm over here on my side, thinking. Seem like there's room for two or three people in between. Like his momma for one, who seemed to have a pretty hard time letting go. Thought her little pinched-in face was going to turn itself inside out yesterday. Enough to make me feel sorry for her.

We're in this nice motel, or maybe hotel, I'm not all that clear on the difference, in Charleston. Just for two nights. Had a bottle of champagne waiting on us when we got here last night after the wedding, and there's a complimentary breakfast included in the price. I sure am glad, on account of I'm getting hungry enough to eat a four-by-four, which is what they call the he-man breakfast they serve down at Whistler's Drive-in where I work—worked, that is, up till Friday.

This isn't our real honeymoon. Jimmy Lee says maybe we'll do that later, go to Disneyworld or something, but right now his daddy needs him in the store since his brother Ham's in Vietnam and Mr. Turner can't handle everything alone. Jimmy Lee had to quit college because of it, he only went two years, but said that's about all he wanted to go anyhow. Rest of what he needs to know he can learn down at the store, he says.

Jimmy Lee won't have to go in the service on account of his asthma. His momma says she's almost lost him she doesn't know how many times. Though how you could misplace anybody that snores this loud is beyond me.

My daddy used to snore something awful, too, before he died. Momma'd sent him out to the couch when she couldn't take it anymore, saying if she didn't get some sleep she wouldn't be worth shooting.

Can't imagine doing something like that to Jimmy Lee. Don't know him well enough. Course, I know a good bit more than I used to, after last night.

He's stirring some now, turned halfway over toward me. Hair's sticking straight out on one side and he looks cute, like a rumpled little boy. I'm lonely way over here and getting hungrier by the minute, so I whisper, Jimmy Lee, Jimmy Lee. He doesn't hear me though. Starts back in on that snoring. It's even louder than Daddy's, almost a cartoon snore. Lord, I reckon that'll take some getting used to.

Getting used to things is something I know how to do. Learned it from watching other people, I reckon, especially Momma, who once said, among other things, a woman's main job in this world is to take what's on her plate and make it taste good. So far the best meal I can make of Jimmy Lee's snoring is to reckon it'll give me plenty of hours lying in bed awake. Good opportunities for thinking. Which on the other hand could be a mixed blessing.

One thing I didn't learn about from Momma was sex, past her mentioning not to do it, that is. Already got my own theories about it, though. Strikes me as one of those things where the buildup is the main part, like the pure pleasure of licking on a lollipop, which is gone the second you lose your head and bite it.

Momma couldn't come to the wedding yesterday. She wanted to, planned to right up to the last minute, but then Mr. Jackson said it was just too far for her to drive herself and he couldn't get time off, being he just started his new job down there and, besides, wasn't anybody to leave the kids with. She told all that in a rush, so quick I couldn't get a word in, finishing up with, "I wanted to be there, Sister. Even bought me a new dress for it."

I didn't say anything, picturing all the words I might say but couldn't, traveling three hundred and some miles over the telephone wire between us, imagining what would happen when they got to her side.

Finally she said, "I'm doing the best I can."

I said, "I know it, Momma. That's fine."

Anyhow, it'd of been awkward for her yesterday, being the only one from my family, outnumbered by that Turner clan. Not that they turned out in force— just Mr. and Mrs. Turner and Celeste, who's married to Jimmy Lee's brother Ham, plus half another in her belly, where she's carrying the second Turner grand-child, an event they view as just short of the Second Coming. Still, that's enough of them to be over-powering.

Wasn't in church, just the Turners' living room, which was plenty fine enough to suit me, though I would've enjoyed starting my walk at the top of their grand staircase, which I had mentioned to Jimmy Lee. His momma, however, said there wasn't any need to start anywhere but from the hall door. *Discreet* is the word I overheard her use to describe how she wanted the wedding handled. That is, once she accepted there wasn't a thing in this world she could do to stop it, an idea she did not welcome with what you'd call good grace.

Jimmy Lee picked me up yesterday at the apart-ment Momma got for me whenever they left. "Just for a month, Sister. Then y'all will have your own place." I can't get over that idea, having my own place.

Momma, on the other hand, couldn't get over the fact that Jimmy Lee Turner'd asked me to marry him. "Didn't this all work out perfect?" She asked me that over and over, shaking her head and marveling at the wonder of it, practically beside herself with delight.

The Turners were beside themselves, too, I reckon. Yesterday, judging from their expressions, you'd of thought it was a funeral going on, and them losing their best friend, instead of, as they say, gaining a daughter. Although not so much Jimmy Lee's daddy as his momma. She was civil, I'll give her that, tried to go through all the motions, face froze up in a pale mask, looking like it'd shatter into a thousand pieces if she's forced to smile. Which there wasn't any danger of.

"Reverend Wilkerson"—she had my upper arm held in a death-grip with her scrawny little bird fingers and I could smell the dry, papery scent of her—"this is . . ."

Her mouth opened, her lips worked, but words failed her, so I stuck my hand out and murmured, "Jimmy Lee's intended," and found myself half-curtseying, which was hazardous, my knees not being steady as they could be.

Reverend Wilkerson's heavy face creased in what must pass with Episcopalians for a smile, and he crunched my hand once, hard and fast enough to make me wince. Jimmy Lee came and got me then, stood me over by Celeste, who kept her mouth shut and her nose pointed up in the air. Then he went back to hovering over by his daddy, who kept talking about Ham the whole time, like he was the one whose day this was, instead of Jimmy Lee. Still, Mr. Turner was about the friendliest one there, besides Jimmy Lee, that is.

Wasn't anybody to give me away, so Reverend Wilkerson said we could dispense with that part. He said his words and we said ours, me cutting my eyes sideways at Jimmy Lee, who never looked anywhere but straight ahead, dead pale as his momma. Then he kissed me—a quick, dry peck I hardly felt—and his momma started bustling around the house, sniffing, picking things up, washing dishes. Whenever we drove off, nobody threw rice or tied stuff to our car, so to me it felt like just another date, only we drove further.

Last night when we got to our room, I noticed the bottle of champagne right off. Turned around to say to Jimmy Lee wasn't that the nicest thing, and when I did, he put his arms around me and started pushing toward the bed, pulling at the jacket of my new aqua pique going-away suit, which he got for me at a real good discount, down at the store—his wedding gift to me, which I thought was sweet.

In my head I'd pictured candlelight, music, and sweet, slow kisses for this part. But I reckon I know desperation when I see it, so I tried to relax and let Jimmy Lee have his way before he hurt himself. My new bra about gave him a fit, and he poked a hole in one of my brand-new stockings, getting it loose from the garter belt. Eventually, however, he did manage to get both our clothes off, except for his socks, which weren't in the way anyhow.

Before I could hardly remember how it felt, it was over. Jimmy Lee heaved himself up and down a few times, our stomachs slapping together with a wet, sticky sound, then he just laid flat on top of me. His heart was beating like a train, I could feel it against mine, which was barely stirred. He was heavy and sweaty. I wanted to be polite, let him rest, but my breath was coming short from his weight on my chest, plus my left foot was asleep, the numbness threatening to climb on up my leg any minute.

"Jimmy Lee, I can't hardly breathe," I said, in a pretty sweet voice, I thought, all things considered. So in a minute he got up and went to the bathroom, me laying in the bed, watching him go, naked as a baby, except for those long black socks wrinkled down around his ankles. Which made my throat lump up, for no good reason.

When he came out, I went in and cleaned him off me. Expected to see more blood — always heard good girls give up buckets of it — but there wasn't much. It is surprising, though, how messy the whole thing is.

Course I know the best thing about it. The point of it. And I'm planning on having a house full, five or six or more. Seem like I've been waiting all my life for that. Got to be around babies a lot when Momma kept a few in our house, that time we lived in Dorchester County. Lord, I loved everything about them, the smell and feel and look and sound of them.

Couldn't wait to get home from school then, play with those babies before their mommas'd come and take them home. You're going to make some wonderful momma, they'd all say that to me, smiling and shaking their heads. I will, too.

What's funny is, I pretty much know all those Turners think that's the reason Jimmy Lee married me—caught his momma cutting her eyes at my belly more than once yesterday. Maybe even my own momma thinks it. They'll find out soon enough, I reckon. No sense trying to tell them anything.

Last night, when I came out the bathroom after cleaning up, Jimmy Lee called me over to the bed, put his arm around me and said he loved me, which made me feel a good bit better. A rerun of *The Virginian* was on, so we sat there and watched that a while, then got dressed, went downstairs and had us a big steak dinner, right here in this hotel. With two glasses of red wine, which was pretty romantic and made my head swimmy.

Minute we got back to the room, Jimmy Lee said for me to go put on that black lace negligee he got me at the store while he opened the bottle of champagne. I didn't think I could drink anything else right then, but I didn't want to be rude. So I got my gown and went to the bathroom, figuring I'd take my time going back out.

Putting that negligee on and looking at myself in the mirror, I started thinking about how it felt when Bobby McAllister touched me. Been trying not to think of him much, but it was hard. Couple weeks after we broke up, I heard from a friend that he'd joined the Navy. Shipped out, by now. And when I try to remember the way things happened, doesn't seem to me like I ever made a real choice between him and Jimmy Lee. It's just how things worked out.

Anyhow, I was wondering if maybe Jimmy Lee'd go slower, now he'd got that first time out of his system. Maybe he could run his hands lightly all over me, make my body tingle and ache, the way I dreamed of.

Dabbed some perfume behind my ears, in the hollow of my neck and behind my knees, which this article I read calls a woman's sensual pulse points. Brushed my hair over to one side so it hung across my face. Jimmy Lee had the radio on, and in a minute I thought he must have turned the TV back on too, because there was a lot of noise out there. Right before I opened the door, I leaned over close to the mirror and smiled to myself, trying out a sexy one.

When I opened the door, I sure was surprised to see Jimmy Lee with four other people, standing over by the table where our bottle of champagne was, laughing and drinking beer. Right off I recognized Jimmy Lee's friend Jack Simonson, a stuck-up kind of boy I never had liked, and his girlfriend Lucy. The other couple I'd never seen before.

"Why, don't she look purty," Jack said, saying it like that just to be ugly, meaning it as some kind of slap at me, holding his beer can up in a salute. They all laughed, and Jimmy Lee said weren't they just too much, he couldn't believe these fools had driven all this way down here for a joke. Said for me to put my robe on and have a beer.

I did, then sat on the bed, holding a beer can in my hand. After about an hour, the two girls got to looking uncomfortable and talked the boys into leaving. Jimmy Lee came back from the door, shaking his head and laughing at the funny remarks Jack and that other boy were yelling down the hall.

It was late. *Wrestle Mania* was on. We watched for a while, till Jimmy Lee finished his beer. The second go-round of sex took a little longer than the first, and this snoring commenced shortly after.

The ceiling tiles in here have sparkles in them, which I didn't notice last night. Stardust.

I let my right foot travel across this huge bed, and when it's stretched out full-length, it finally touches my husband's leg under the covers. I give the slightest push—not really a kick, more like a little nudge. Because this boy's got to wake up. I am hungry as all get-out.

Twenty-One

Lord, my head aches. Can't much open my eyes. I slit
them up tiny, like a China woman's, which sometimes makes things clearer, but this morning it
doesn't work. Everything's gritty, like it's covered in
sand. That's how my mouth feels, too, like I could
spit and spit and never get the dirt out.

We celebrated last night, Jimmy Lee and me. It was
his idea. Let's go to the beach for your birthday, sugar,
he said, the day before. About stunned me speechless. We hadn't been anywhere in ages, and I don't
know the last time Jimmy Lee called me sugar.

Had a big fight, week before last. I reckon this is his
way of trying to make up. Boy doesn't know how to
say sorry in plain English.

Sure does know how to snore, though. Every time
he takes one of those huge in-breaths over there on
his side of the bed, I cringe, knowing what's coming.

When there's a long quiet spell, I hold my breath, too. This morning it hurts my head more, listening.

Never have been able to drink champagne. Always reminds me of our honeymoon.

Hadn't been to Charleston since then, either, till yesterday. Yesterday what we did is packed us a picnic lunch and drove up here from Red Hill, which is about two hours. Jimmy Lee must of already had this place in mind—Folly Beach, just outside the city— because he didn't ask my opinion about where to stay. It's pretty nice, right on the beach, with sliding glass doors that open up to the sand. Not a high-rise, though, which I would've voted for, if I was asked, because I never stayed in one of them, and I bet you can see a lot from up there.

Whenever we got here, first thing we did was put on our bathing suits, which mine was new, white with electric blue sideways stripes. It was a present from Jimmy Lee, got it for me down at the store. A Jantzen, which I always wanted. Course it was on sale, this being October, and he got our usual discount, so I figure it didn't cost him more than five or six dollars. And it's one size smaller than it should be, which makes me feel like I got two sets of cheeks, one covered and one un. Jimmy Lee says he likes it like that, which makes me wonder how come he doesn't wear *his* that way.

Soon's we got checked in, we went out on the beach and sat in little chairs we brought which Jimmy Lee borrowed from Ham. He and Celeste have a house full of things they never use, like little beach chairs and fondue sets. We ate the cheese and crackers I brought and Jimmy Lee drank beer, which I had one too, but then I got cold. Sun was shining but the wind bit some. We were almost the only people out there, a weekday in October not exactly being prime beach time. It was a perfect opportunity to talk, maybe get a few things straight. But every time I opened my mouth to start, Jimmy Lee'd heave a big sigh, like he was the most put-upon thing in this world. It was his day off, he said, and my birthday. Couldn't we just relax and enjoy it? Drink up, he said. You're legal.

It doesn't feel a bit different, being twenty-one. Funny how I always looked forward to it, thinking it would. Maybe when I get to vote next month it will, although Jimmy Lee says there's not much to it—just pulling one lever, on account of Turners always vote a straight ticket.

Anyhow, I did like Jimmy Lee suggested—proceeded to drink up, after I got something to cover me, that is. Sat on that beach in the sun and the wind in my new bathing suit with a blanket around me and drank beer with my husband. Which may sound like fun but wasn't. I don't know what he was thinking about because he didn't say, but I was thinking about that fight we had.

Must be how come I answered him so ugly whenever he asked did I want to go into Charleston and walk around, look at old houses. That, and the beer, which makes me mean sometimes. At which point he got huffy, saying here he was, putting himself out for me, he thought I loved looking at old things, there was plenty else he'd rather be doing on his day off. I said I was sorry, and I was, it's not how I usually act. Jimmy Lee sulked a while but got over it. We changed clothes and went into the city.

Right about then's when the day started taking its turn towards good. I mean, the sun was glinting off the church spires when we were driving over that high bridge into Charleston, the Cooper River stretched out long below, tiny ships moving around down there in the water. Then a seagull flew eye-level with our car for a minute. He was greeting us, I figured, saying welcome. That made me feel full and happy, and I leaned over and gave Jimmy Lee a big one, right on the cheek. Which surprised him, I could tell.

It was like something you might read about, after that. We walked a while, then Jimmy Lee saw me looking at one of those old-timey carriages they show people around in and asked did I want to go on one. Yes, I did. We sat up front, right behind the driver, Mary Lynn, a cute little girl who was working her way through the College of Charleston by giving tours. She told us stories about the houses and who used to live there and who did now. Mostly it's still all the old families who've been living in Charleston since it was invented. Blue bloods. I kept hoping to catch sight of one, but didn't, not that I know of. Midway through the ride, Charlie, that was Mary Lynn's horse, developed a terrible stomach ailment. Started breaking wind about every other stride. He'd heave his tail up and wave it, just before. Fair warning. Mary Lynn didn't say a word, so we didn't either, though between the smell and the noise it was impossible to ignore. Jimmy Lee and I got so tickled we didn't hardly hear the last part of her talk.

After the ride, we went to this Mexican restaurant named Garcia's, ordered tacos with a side of refried beans and margaritas with lots of salt. I was hoping they'd ask for my ID, but they didn't. Still, I believe it was the best meal I ever ate. Looking over at Jimmy Lee across the candle on our table, I felt grown-up and happy.

It was getting dark. We walked through the market, looking at the basket weavers and the bright vegetable stands. We were both a little tight, I reckon, but ready for more. Jimmy Lee said I had to have champagne. You're only twenty-one once, he said, so he stopped in at a corner red dot and bought us some. We walked to our car, where he sat down, held the bottle between his knees, and opened it with a loud pop. We stayed there and drank some, right out the bottle. I wasn't thinking anymore about champagne being my unlucky drink.

The curve of the day started going the other way, near as I can figure, when Jimmy Lee asked did I want to go see a movie. Course I did, I love movies, didn't even think to ask which one. He walked me down King to Coming Street. We took a turn off there, and here was this seedy-looking little theater. Adult shows nightly, according to the sign over the pictures of a bunch of half-naked, long-haired women.

Here's the part I can't figure: he had to know I wasn't going to like it. It's what we been fighting about. So why'd he do it? Just when things were going like they were. Momma used to say, men are a puzzlement, remember that. But I don't know what good remembering it is, if there's nothing you can do about it.

I put my hands on my hips right there on the sidewalk and asked Jimmy Lee had he lost his mind. He took me off to one side, right under the ADULTS ONLY, ID REQUIRED sign, he said, sugar, just this once, just you and me this time, nobody in there knows us, you'll like it, it's kind of like art, give it a chance, you never give anything a chance, it's your birthday, please. And I don't know if it was him calling me sugar again, or the champagne, or the desperation in his voice, but I said yes.

Inside, it wasn't a thing like a real theater. Didn't even have a snack stand. I figured maybe people who went to those kinds of movies were hungry for something else, or didn't want to break their concentration, munching on things and slurping Coke while they watched. Else maybe they needed their hands free.

It was so dark past that curtain, I couldn't see Jimmy Lee. The place had a musty, used-up smell. Once my eyes adjusted, I saw five or six people, all men, spaced far apart as they could get. The movie hadn't started. There was no music, no coming attractions, no pictures of Coke and popcorn. It was so quiet you could hear people's eyes blink. I was grateful for the darkness but wished for some background noise. Didn't care to hear strangers breathing hard.

For that matter, I'm not crazy about hearing people I know breathe hard. Which is what started that fight two weeks ago. We'd been over to Jim Bennett's house, he's a friend of Jimmy Lee's, and he's OK, not stuck-up like some of them. But his wife, Corky—can you believe that, a grown woman named Corky?— she is. Stuck-up, snooty, carried away with herself. Thinks she's sexy, too. You can tell it by how she moves her lips more than she needs to when she talks. There was a group of us there, a party. We don't go to many of them, I just can't get comfortable, the men go off in one room, usually the kitchen, where the bar is, and the women in another. The men talk low in there, I don't know about what, and laugh loud every once in a while. The women talk about their babies or their jobs or their colleges, which pretty much leaves me out cold, and sometimes they get to talking about *All My Children* or *Love of Life,* but I never have much cared for soaps. They don't seem real. I'd just as soon play solitaire or work a jigsaw puzzle when I got time on my hands.

I keep telling Jimmy Lee I want a job, I even have one in mind I know I could get, but he says it just wouldn't look right, his wife working like that. All it is is working down at the Methodist Church nursery, helping out with the babies in the mornings. They need an assistant then and Mrs. Laurette says I'd be perfect for it, but Jimmy Lee says, first off, we're

Episcopalians, and second, he wants me here when he comes home for lunch, and thirdly . . . well, by the time he gets to thirdly I know I lost anyway, so I quit listening. But if I had a job, maybe I'd have something to talk about. Or a baby. Which is another problem altogether.

Anyhow, this party seemed like all the rest, everybody separated up, till around ten o'clock Corky pipes up and says, "Jimbo, how about that movie now?" She's the only one ever calls her husband Jimbo, and the way she says it makes me sick, but he doesn't seem to mind. The men start laughing louder than usual and the women get quiet and I'm waiting for somebody to turn on the TV, figure a good movie's coming on. Even when Jim brings out the projector, I'm still in the dark, thinking, oh, home movies. The title flashes up on the screen, *The Fuller Brushman Cometh,* and there's a housewife opening her door and the salesman comes in and starts demonstrating his brushes and then she goes to ogling him like she's got something in her eye and he looks back and by this time I'm realizing it's not Corky and Jim's summer vacation in Florida. I punch Jimmy Lee in the ribs with my elbow and whisper, let's go home, and he pats my hand once or twice, but doesn't answer me or tear his eyes off that screen. Then, louder, I say, let's go home, and this time he turns his head a little my way and says, shhh. I watch a minute more, then stand up. My shadow blocks the picture and somebody says, for God's sake, get her down. I squat and watch one more scene, then scoot out to the hall on my fanny, get my pocketbook and start walking.

I was about a mile down the road when Jimmy Lee picked me up. I could tell how mad he was by the sound of his tires when he hit the brakes, but he didn't say a word till we got in the house. Then he let go. You know how fights start out about one thing and lead to everything else? — that's how this one went. Started out him saying I was a prude, a baby, when was I going to grow up? So then I asked him since when was watching dirty movies with a bunch of other people in somebody's living room a sign of being grown. And how grown up was he, I said, a boy who still has breakfast with his momma every morning of his life and works for his daddy. He said I was suppressed something terrible and he was trying to help me and I asked him, help me what, have sex with a door-to-door brush salesman? He said he'd be happy for me to do that if it'd make me loosen up, and how, he hollered, did I ever expect to have babies if we never had sex. That quieted me down. I was ready to quit then, but he wasn't. He went on and on, finally said why couldn't I be like other women, what was wrong with me. He had me there. I said I didn't know.

I was all of a sudden tired and went on into the bedroom. He followed me. I got undressed while he watched me and then I lay in the bed. He came over and put his hand on me and it felt more like a slab of stone or dead flesh than living skin. After a minute he took it away and told me I was frigid. Soon as he said it I knew it must be so because I felt cold from the inside out.

He slept on the couch that night, and I slept in our bed, holding onto my own arms to keep from shivering to death. Next day he didn't mention it. That's how he usually does, thinks things go away by themselves. We had sex that night, so I reckon he figured it worked.

Maybe it did, too. Because he's right. I know we can't have babies unless we have sex, and I do want them, and it must be my fault we haven't yet since for some reason I don't know I don't even like to think about having sex with Jimmy Lee. I'd rather scrub floors. It's less tiresome.

It's OK being Jimmy Lee's wife in other ways, though. I'm learning to be a pretty good cook and I don't mind picking up after him and doing laundry. After all, like he says, he's the one out there earning our living. I just wish there was another way to have a baby and satisfy Jimmy Lee at the same time, but I don't know of one.

So all that's going through my mind when we took our seats in that theater last night. Jimmy Lee's trying to help me, I know that, he says I'm pent-up, sexiness is smoldering inside me somewhere, he's read articles about it. I have, too. *Reader's Digest* almost always has one about six steps to keeping your spouse happy, which is another way of saying sex, but I can't ever figure how to apply those steps to me and Jimmy Lee.

I took a deep breath, but quiet, didn't want to call attention to myself, and sat back against the seat, just as the reel started rolling and the title flashed across the screen.

I could tell right off this one was classier than the Fuller Brush one. It was in color and had music, which I was glad of, because it took care of that background noise. Title wasn't bad either, just people's names: *Jack and Jill and Hilda.* Jill and Hilda showed up on the screen first thing, two big-bosomed, good-looking women, a blonde and a brunette. I noticed their mouths weren't moving with the words, which meant it was foreign, probably French, which made me think maybe Jimmy Lee was right about it being art. They're hiking through the woods, and meet up with Jack, a little guy with a thin mustache, walking his dog, a Great Dane he can't hardly keep on the leash.

From there things went straight downhill. It was a mishmash of nursery rhymes and fairy tales gone crazy: Little Red Riding Hood, the wolf and her grandmother got surprisingly friendly, after which Snow White entertained the Seven Dwarfs in the little cottage she'd just cleaned up. I believe I recognized two of those dwarfs from *The Wizard of Oz,* which just didn't seem right. But after I got over being so shocked by what they were doing, I got tickled. It was nothing but pure silly. I couldn't figure how they kept their faces straight. Looked over at Jimmy Lee, but he wasn't laughing. When they got to the part about Bo Peep and her sheep, I couldn't contain myself— laughed out loud, said to Jimmy Lee, reckon how they train them to do that?

Six heads swiveled my way. I quit laughing. Jimmy Lee got me up by one arm and pushed me out of there ahead of him, kind of hissing under his breath. I glanced back just as Little Boy Blue was fixing to blow his horn. Must not've had a bone in his body.

In the car on the way back to the motel, I tried to tease Jimmy Lee out of it, telling him at least I sat through it, couldn't he see how it was funny? But he wouldn't say a word, not till we got to the motel, then he turned off the car, looked over at me and said, I give up. He got out and went in, not looking back.

That's when I grabbed the champagne bottle out the car and drank the rest of it, walking along the beach, celebrating with the moon, which is why I reckon I feel sick this morning. Else maybe it's because I'm getting ready to start, should've last week and didn't. Else maybe this is just how being grown up feels.

Moving On

"Always knew it'd end up like this." That's what I tell Jimmy Lee, talking about Thomas.

He doesn't answer me; just grunts under his breath, which I really hate.

We're getting dressed. I'm trying to pull my pantyhose over my upper legs, which is not as easy as it used to be. I'm bending over and a little out of breath. Durn things are creasing up on me. I'm trying not to pull too hard because they'll run and there's $3.89 plus tax down the tubes because these are the good ones since we're going to church and all.

Thomas is . . . keep saying that, can't seem to get it through my head. Thomas *was* this boy Jimmy Lee knew practically all his life, who I got to know after Jimmy Lee and I got married, who lived next door to us for three years when we rented that place over in the Baytown section. Day we heard Thomas and his wife Celia were buying the house next door, I remember I said to Jimmy Lee: Jimmy Lee, let's move. I don't remember what he said back, but we didn't.

He's gone into the kitchen now, looking for something to eat. We're ready too early, as usual. So I reckon he's going to wolf down anything he can find loose in the fridge. Does that when he's nervous. Even if we weren't ready early and didn't have this extra time on our hands to kill and didn't have stuff to think about we wish we didn't, he'd still be in there rummaging through the cupboards like some kind of stray dog hungry for scraps. I wish he wouldn't, but I'd be wasting my breath telling him that because Jimmy Lee just ignores me when I try to change his bad habits by calling attention to them.

First time I ever remember hearing about Thomas, it was something bad. Jimmy Lee and I'd only been married about a year and so I guess Thomas and Celia had too, since we all got married the same year. I didn't know them then, but later it struck me funny, how we got married the same year in the same little town, then ended up living next door to each other. It probably isn't that funny, but I'm one who's always looking for little things that connect together, you know? In ways you don't see till later? Drives Jimmy Lee slam up the wall.

Anyhow, what I heard was—and I heard it from Leila Anne Morrison, who was right there while it was happening, so I know it's true—she said Thomas beat Celia up. In a boat. While Leila Anne and her date Bo Tucker sat there watching. It was awful. They'd been drinking a good bit, they were on their way back from Goat Island. Celia was complaining about Thomas flirting with some girl on the beach. Leila Anne said Celia went on and on, kind of whining, not letting up for a second. Thomas wasn't saying anything much. Tried to kid her out of it at first and then clammed up. Leila Anne said Celia wouldn't quit. It was getting on her nerves, she was about to tell her to shut up herself, and then, so fast Leila Anne said it didn't register till later, Thomas's hand shot out and smacked Celia in the mouth. Didn't shut her up, though. Her voice just got higher and louder. Leila Anne looked at Thomas and his eyes went kind of dead and he stood over Celia and hit her in the face back and forth with the flat of his hand, first with the palm and then with the back.

Leila Anne said she couldn't move. Bo was driving the boat and Celia was cussing and screaming. Then Bo turned the motor off and went for Thomas, who never even turned around, just planted his feet harder and kept on backing and forthing at Celia's face. Bo grabbed him from behind and heaved him over the side. He came up sputtering and looking startled, like he'd just woke up. Leila Anne said Bo's back was to Celia. He was looking at Thomas there in the water—trying to figure what to do next, I guess—when Celia jumped him from behind and started beating on his back with her fists and screaming at him not to hurt her husband. Leila Anne said if she hadn't been in such a state of shock she might have laughed. By the time Thomas got back in the boat,

Celia was cooing and murmuring over him like he
was a lost baby or something. Leila Anne said she
didn't plan on going off with them again. Who could
blame her, I said, and made up my mind to steer
clear of those two.

When I told Jimmy Lee about it, he wasn't surprised. Said Thomas had always been strange, then
when he came back from Vietnam, he passed from
strange into crazy. Got some kind of medal there,
Jimmy Lee said, and also some kind of plate inside
his head. Medal for metal. Ha. But Jimmy Lee said
that wasn't what made Thomas strange. Said he'd
always been that way. He was just a little stranger,
after.

Take his name, for instance. Full name was Thomas
Joseph Jordan. Pronounced Jerdan. That's a big deal
here, whether you call it Jor or Jer. To me it's funny,
because neither one of them carries any weight in
Red Hill, but to a Jordan it's dead serious. That's not
even the part I mean, though. I mean, Thomas. Not
Tommy or Tommy Joe or TJ, like you'd expect.
Thomas. Like he thought that could make up for the
Jordan part. As if anything could. Around here, nothing makes up for not having the right name. Turners
and Middletons just don't marry Jordans. Not and
live happily ever after. Celia's a Middleton, and even
though she hung that same middle name on both her
girls, they still got to drag that Jordan name along
behind it. Bet she hopes they marry early.

"How about leave that ham alone, Jimmy Lee.
That's for tonight." He's really rooting around in there

now, talking ugly at me under his breath, too. Nerves are shot.

There'll be plenty to eat at the house. I think of telling him that, but don't because he might not can take it. I sent over a ham and my carrot cake. Thought that was a good bit, considering we haven't seen Thomas and Celia for over five years, not to do more than just speak, that is.

Almost sent a crab casserole, without thinking, I guess. That would've been funny. Celia'd probably never of known, her momma or somebody'll likely write the thank-yous for her. But still. It would've been funny, see, because Thomas is the one who taught me to pick crab. Course, I never could do it like him. Nobody could. Lord, his fingers flew so fast you couldn't see what he was doing. He had to slow it down to teach me.

How I got from wanting to move out because Thomas and Celia bought the house next door to learning to pick crab from him, I don't exactly know.

I'd been dreading their moving in, as I say, staying up nights worrying about loud fights next door and till all hours of the night partying and so forth. That day I was out in the yard doing something, pruning shrubs maybe, and keeping my eye on the truck. You can tell a lot about people from their furniture, I always say, and I got to admit I was curious. Theirs was about what you'd expect, a few good pieces, probably Celia's momma's, and the rest kind of junky. Jimmy Lee and I didn't have living room furniture yet. I was saving up for something good, and like I told him, I'd rather have an empty room than stick tacky furniture in there till we can afford the right stuff. He said he'd rather have something to sit on, good or not. I know he's glad now I won that argument. Every time I pass by our living room and look in I get a thrill of pride. Course, we don't ever really sit in there, except for bridge club.

Anyhow, that day I was kind of working in the yard, like I said. And for a minute I guess I really did get to working because all of a sudden I look up and there's Thomas, standing about a foot away. I hadn't heard him at all. He's just looking at me and right away I notice his eyes because they're different, a little almondy-shaped and kind of gold-colored with flecks of black in them and he's looking at me so hard I feel like he knows what I'm thinking. I drop the clippers and they land on my toe.

So that's how we first met, my big toe cut open and him so sweet and quick about putting Merthiolate on it and wrapping it up and me crying because it hurt so bad and embarrassed about him touching my feet. I always hated my feet.

In a minute Celia came over with her two girls, Sally and Lucy, and her momma. Mrs. Middleton was a thin, sharp-faced woman, with a nose that looked like it could chop wood. Made me think to myself if I had to look like that to be a Middleton, I was just as glad not to be one. She acted pretty nice, considering, but I could see her measuring me, peering in at our empty living room and maybe at my feet. She looked at me the way Jimmy Lee's momma always does. It's a look people like Turners and Middletons got down pat. Maybe they're born with it.

Anyhow, by the time Jimmy Lee got home from work, Mrs. Middleton was gone, Thomas had bought two six-packs of beer, and the three of us—Celia, Thomas, and me—were having a high old time. Jimmy Lee joined right in, and all of a sudden the thing I'd been dreading so hard had turned into a party.

Not that Celia and Thomas didn't have problems. They did. She was crazy jealous, and though she didn't have her momma's sharp face, her tongue was razor-quick and mean. Not always, of course, just when she'd been drinking and he'd been flirting. Which was a lot. Thomas was a terrible flirt. Seemed like he just couldn't help himself. And though he certainly wasn't my type—he was dark, like me, had those funny eyes and skin that in summer turned a deep, golden brown, whereas I like blonds with blue eyes, like Jimmy Lee and Robert Redford—still, there was something about him. Thomas was kind of overweight, too, had this beer gut, but it didn't in the least embarrass him. Went around all the time without a shirt on, like he was proud of it. I do remember that the skin of his belly looked so smooth it made your fingers itch to touch it.

It was spring of the second year, I think, when Thomas decided I needed to learn to pick crab. He loved doing it, would sit for hours at their kitchen table, drinking one beer after another, fingers flying, making a mound of crab meat. Then he'd put some

butter in a big iron skillet and dump the crab in and
sauté it real quick and we'd stand around, eat it right
out of the pan. Lord, I don't know if anything has
tasted that sweet since.

Once he offered me some from his fingers, being
funny, I guess. I don't know where Jimmy Lee and
Celia had got to just then. I looked up and he was
studying me with those gold-flecked eyes of his and I
kept looking and opened my mouth and took it. And
if I close my eyes right now while I lie here face up on
my bed in the middle of the day dressed fit to kill and
waiting to go see Thomas one last time, I can still
taste that sweet hot crab meat on my tongue and feel
the smooth warm tips of his fingers against my lips.
Got a feeling in my belly I hadn't had since before I
got married. Made me know how come Celia'd married him.

I never saw Thomas hit her. After while, I put that
Leila Anne Morrison story right out of my mind.
Sometimes, though, I'd see that flatness come into
his eyes, when Celia'd go on and on about something, and once when I came up behind him unex-
pectedly. When I touched him that time, he jumped
and turned and his eyes were black, seem like, and
dead. Gave back no light or something. I don't know.
Don't like to think of it.

But mostly Thomas seemed happy. Looking back, I
think those must have been the best years he and
Celia had. They were past that crazy early stage and
not yet into the one I heard about later, when she'd
have to take the girls every once in a while and spend

a few days at her momma's because he'd gone off the deep end again. Maybe it had to do with that plate in his head, or maybe it was just Thomas. How could anybody have known it, I ask Jimmy Lee. You can probably guess what he answers. Boy doesn't hear half I say.

The last year we lived in Baytown, though, things did start on a downturn. That was the year I lost the baby. Nobody could have been any sweeter to me than Thomas and Celia were then. Celia fixed supper about every night. Thomas came over to visit during the day and we'd talk and talk. It was surprising, how much we had in common. He sure could make me laugh. He worked shift work at the paper mill, so his hours changed every week, whereas you could set your watch by Jimmy Lee's comings and goings, working down at his daddy's store.

Jimmy Lee didn't know what to say to me anyhow. He always hated me to cry, made him feel helpless and mad. Once, a week or so after losing the baby, I was lying in bed half asleep, kept hearing a funny sound over and over, coming from the bathroom. Jimmy Lee wasn't in bed, even though it was past midnight. I got up and crept down the hall. The bathroom door was cracked open; I could see through it. There sat Jimmy Lee on the potty seat, holding a towel up over his face. The noise was coming from him. I stood there in the shadows a while, watching through the crack of the door, but I couldn't make a word come out of my mouth. Then I went on back to bed, turned on the TV, and fell asleep. Later on that night, Jimmy Lee's snoring woke me, like it will sometimes. I went in the bathroom and got that towel out the dirty clothes hamper. Held it up to my face a while, then put it back. It was a pink one, with flowers.

I guess Jimmy Lee felt like I did, that I was a failure. I know his momma did, because I heard she said, wasn't bad enough Jimmy Lee had to go marry somebody like me, looked like I wasn't even going to be able to have babies right. Doc Logan said, after the DNC, it was a miracle I ever got pregnant in the first place.

It was about two months after that—late spring, a Saturday afternoon, and Celia and Thomas and me sitting in our front yard having a few beers, waiting for Jimmy Lee to get off work—when Jack Simonson came wheeling up in his shiny new Corvette and parked it right on our grass. Don't know why Jimmy Lee keeps Jack for a friend. He's the kind of boy who's always puffed up with himself, the kind who's always driving something like a shiny new Corvette. Sure enough, he was drunk, obnoxious, loud. His usual self. Came swaggering over, plopped down, helped himself to one of our beers without asking and proceeded to hog the conversation. Celia didn't mind him, I could tell. Thomas tensed up at first, then relaxed. I could see him making himself do that.

Jack has this irritating habit of clearing his throat about every other sentence and then kind of snorting. Drives me plumb crazy. So in a minute he cleared his throat once, turned to me, snorted, and said something about too bad I couldn't seem to have babies, did I think Jimmy Lee'd go out and find him a woman who could? I was so surprised I couldn't talk, and for some stupid reason I started to cry. Thomas stood up, his lawn chair flipped over backwards, and he said in a very soft voice that Jack had better leave. Jack sputtered, said he was just kidding, he didn't mean anything by it. But he went on over to his car, not taking his eyes off Thomas. Thomas stood by my chair with his hands on his hips, watching. When Jack got to his car, he turned around, gave Thomas the finger, said fuck you, buddy, then got in his car and gunned it.

Well, we'd had a lot of rain that spring and the front yard was pretty well saturated. The back wheels of Jack's Corvette spun around, dug in, and held. He slung mud and grass everywhere. His car didn't budge.

Thomas was beside me one instant and the next he was at Jack Simonson's car, had jerked the door open and pulled Jack out by the throat with one hand. With the fist of the other he hit him right in the face three or four times. Quick, hard jabs. Jack said nothing; Thomas said nothing. There was no sound at all except the sound of fist on face. Then it was over. Jack slumped in his seat. Thomas walked back to us, eyes flat, fist bloody. He sat down, wiped his hand on the grass, threw his head back, and stared up at the sky. He didn't even glance over toward the road. Celia and I said nothing. Then she got up, opened a beer, and took it over to Thomas.

In a while Jack's car started, backed up a little and then pulled away, very slowly. None of us looked. We just sipped our beers.

By the time Jimmy Lee got home, we'd made a joke out of the whole thing, Jack with his exit line and no place to go. But the deep gouge in our front yard was still there three months later when we moved.

See, Jimmy Lee and I always knew we wouldn't stay in Baytown. That's how come we were renting. It was just a first step for us. Like the empty living room. Thomas and Celia had bought their house, though, like I said. They were staying put. Wouldn't have mattered much to me, Baytown being the nicest place I'd ever lived anyway. But with Celia, it was different. When she chose to marry Thomas, wonder did she know it'd be like that?

About a week before we left, Jimmy Lee and I had supper over at Thomas and Celia's.

I reckon I knew something bad was going to happen because Jimmy Lee and Thomas were drinking bourbon instead of beer. Neither one of them could handle it. Wasn't a thing I could say that'd make a difference, though, I knew that. So I kept my mouth shut. I always wished so bad I had said something and they wouldn't have done it and everything wouldn't have changed like it did. But I didn't. So. Wasn't my place to. A woman's place. Ha. Wonder where in the world that is.

But like I always tell Jimmy Lee, you can't look back. There's just no future in it.

Anyhow, they were drinking bourbon, and Celia and I were drinking beer. We had supper and did the dishes and then sat around in their living room. The girls were in bed and Celia and I were talking about curtains and furniture and shrubbery for the new house—Jimmy Lee's momma got us a good deal on it, the owner being one of her widow friends. It's two blocks from downtown, on St. James Street, the second best area in town, but now Jimmy Lee's getting tired of this, so we just looked at one last week in the country club with four bedrooms and three baths, right on the lake. It's awful big, but I figure we can always close off the extra rooms and use them in case we have company or something. Anyhow, that night Celia had enough upbringing and good taste to act excited about our move. We said we'd miss each other and we'd still get together a lot. I reckon we both knew better.

We'd been sitting an hour or two when there was an awful commotion just outside the house—clanging and barking and screeching. Dogs. See, our street was near the end of the neighborhood, next to some woods, and people'd dump unwanted pets off there. Always had strays around. Our garbage spent more time strewn from here to yonder than it did in the can or the truck, which only came once a week, which just wasn't enough. Comes twice a week at St. James Street. Three times at the country club.

Thomas and Jimmy Lee started cussing those dogs and got up to go chase them off. They were pretty drunk, but I figured, what harm could they do, on foot. They were gone a long time. Came back strange and quiet. In a minute Jimmy Lee said to let's go, so we did.

On the way home, he started crying. I'd never seen him cry before, except maybe that time with the towel, I don't know. By the time I got him in the house, he was blubbering like a baby, trying to talk through it. Couldn't make out what he was saying, at first. Then he told me what Thomas had done, that they'd chased those dogs into the woods and Thomas picked up a stick and hit one of them and it squealed and then Thomas kicked it in the head and it stopped running and the others ran off but that one couldn't and Thomas kicked it again and again. Jimmy Lee said he might have kicked it once or twice too, he didn't know. Then it just lay there, bloody and smashed. Thomas looked at Jimmy Lee and said did he want to know what he did one time in Vietnam. Jimmy Lee must of said yes, because Thomas told him once he raped a woman over there, in her own house in some little village, and maybe he killed her, he didn't know, he had kicked her like a dog when he finished.

Jimmy Lee got quiet after that, but his words hung in the air, making their own terrible pictures and sounds. I could hear kicking boots and screams.

Then Jimmy Lee threw up. I put him to bed and pulled the covers up over his head. Then I pulled them back down because I thought if he smelled his own breath he might throw up again.

But then I couldn't sleep and seem like all the beer I'd drunk hadn't touched me. Couldn't stop thinking about the dog over there in the woods. And the woman. And Thomas.

The living room light was still on next door. It was pitch black and quiet as I walked over. I was all the way under the carport, heading for the side door, when I saw Thomas, sitting on the steps, holding his head in his hands. He heard me coming, I reckon, because he started talking in a low voice, not looking up. I leaned against their car and looked at his outline in the dark while he told me he was sick and he knew it and he didn't know what to do about it. That sometimes he got so mixed up he didn't know what he was doing. Celia thought it would go away, he said. She didn't want people to know, her momma especially.

Thomas Joseph Jordan sat there on that still, black, August night five years ago, naked to the waist, head in his hands, and asked me would it go away. He kept his head down, waiting. Like he thought I had an answer. Part of me wanted to go over to him, stroke his bare skin, touch him in some way, but I couldn't move myself from that car. I was afraid of what might happen. Finally, I told him I didn't know, to get some sleep. I went to bed then.

I never looked Thomas Jordan straight in the eye again. We saw him and Celia the next week, of course, but we were getting ready for the move and just had time to speak or wave and go on about our business. I didn't sleep much that week. I'd lie awake

51

and look at the ceiling and wonder what could I do. Thought about talking to Celia, to Jimmy Lee, to Doc Logan. In the end that's all I did, was thought about it. Jimmy Lee claimed he was so drunk the whole night was a blank. I decided to do like him, act like it never happened.

But all that week I caught a scent of rotting flesh from somewhere in those woods across the way.

After we moved, we didn't see much of Thomas and Celia. They were invited to our housewarming party, and they came, but there was a crowd of people there and we didn't get a chance to talk. Seem like they left early.

After while I started hearing those stories, about Thomas threatening Celia and the girls with a gun, about them going to stay at her momma's, about separations and reconciliations. By that time, we only saw them maybe passing by in the car and once or twice in the grocery store. You know how time gets away from you.

So how surprised should I have been yesterday when Jimmy Lee gets a call from Bo Tucker, telling him about Thomas? About how Thomas and Celia fought again and he'd pulled out his old .357 and she and the girls got into the car, about how he'd stood on the front stoop of that house in Baytown with tears in his eyes and said to come on back in honey and about how she'd almost done it, but then she'd seen something else in his eyes and left instead. She waited for the usual call from him saying he was better, she could come home. Waited two days, then started calling him. Finally called Bo. He got Billy Walker to go over there with him. Door was locked, so they'd walked around to the backyard and looked in the window. The shade was down most of the way, but they could see Thomas's foot lying quiet on the bed. Still had his shoe on. They broke in and found him, head shot all to pieces. A terrible mess. No note.

Funeral's today, Bo said, because it was summer and he'd already been dead two days, and would Jimmy Lee be a pallbearer. Jimmy Lee said he couldn't because of his back.

Keep thinking of Celia and her momma and the girls sitting there in that church, waiting to be finished with Thomas. I bet Jimmy Lee'll want us to sit right behind them. I reckon we will, whether I want to or not. I just don't know anymore.

Time to go now, finally, so I check my makeup in the mirror and it seems fine, though I look funny to myself around the eyes, and I holler to Jimmy Lee that it's time, but he's not even here, he's already out in the yard, hot as it is.

I'm glad it's a closed casket. Who knows what I might see if I had to look on Thomas Joseph Jordan's face again?

"Wasn't anything anybody could've done," I tell Jimmy Lee as we pull out of our drive and into the summer afternoon. My legs already feel tingly from the sweat starting to push through these tight pantyhose. I look in the mirror over the visor and see it beaded on my upper lip. I don't look at my eyes, only at the sweat on my lip. Jimmy Lee just grunts.

Down at the Store

Phone's ringing again. Drives me crazy, how people'll let it ring on and on like that. If I want to talk to you, Delphine Moses, I'll let you know. Don't call me, I'll call you.

"You should see the skirt Stella's got on today, Miss Mattie. She once sits down, it'll be all over." That's the kind of thing Delphine tells me, in that breathy little voice she puts on. Drives me crazy, too, how she calls me that—Miss Mattie. Reckon it's on account of me being married to Jimmy Lee, but I wish she'd quit.

Just about once a day, and sometimes twice, for the past month now, Delphine's been calling me from the dressing room phone—that's her job, dressing room monitor—telling me what all's going on down at the store, talking in a whisper reminds me of an obscene phone caller's. Not that I ever had an obscene phone call, I never did, though Thelma

Sanderson did once, broke it to us at bridge, only telling the first letters and making us guess the rest of the words he whispered while she hung on her side of the phone and listened. Much longer than she should have, if you ask me. Which feelings I naturally kept to myself, while Tootsie Middleton whooped and pressed for details and Ida Jean Munroe turned pale, failed to finesse for Thelma's king of spades, and went down two, her lips thinning near to nothing.

"He's at it again," Delphine'll whisper, and I know who she means is Ham. She hates him for some reason, maybe because he's her boss, the store manager, and a bully; whereas Jimmy Lee's the assistant manager, being the younger brother, and she says he reminds her of a little boy. Not that any of that matters one whit, because even though Mr. Turner's supposedly retired and only there on what he calls a consulting basis, that turns out to be sunup to closing, meaning neither one of those boys is really running the store, regardless of what they might believe, which is part of the problem. Even I can tell that, and I don't know much about what goes on down there, or didn't, till Delphine started her phone campaign.

I don't make a habit of spending time down at the store, partly because Jimmy Lee says he's just as soon I didn't—if I want something, he says, just let him know and he'll see about it—and partly because I'm not partial to Ham myself, and the way people act so sweet to him and play up to his big-shot self makes me sick. Especially Jimmy Lee, who thinks his brother is God's gift or something. Which that makes two of them.

"Tootsie Middleton bought six pairs of Christian Dior undies today—every color we had." That's the kind of news Delphine used to pass on when she first started calling. Why she started is another question altogether. It was after I went down there one day when Jimmy Lee and Ham'd gone to Charleston for some conference. I was exchanging that quilted housecoat Jimmy Lee bought for my birthday, big and stiff enough to make you feel like you're wearing a tent, plus hot as the hinges. Me and Delphine got to talking in the dressing room, me as usual looking at a spot just past her shoulder, trying not to look at her face, thinking to myself she's just lonely.

Truth is, I'd much rather talk to Delphine Moses on the phone than see her in person, on account of how her face is. Jimmy Lee told me she was in a terrible car wreck when she was little, both her momma and daddy died in it, plus a sister or brother, I forget which. Anyhow, her whole face was smashed in and now one side of it lacks a jaw, just slopes from ear straight down to neck, the skin smooth as if she'd been born that way. She has a habit of stroking it from time to time while she talks, like a man with a beard'll do.

"Murph Merchison bought a black lace nightie in a size 6," she whispers, and what we both know and don't have to mention is that his wife Sally's big as a house. "Myrtle Feagin finally gave in, went to a size

16 today." Listening to her whisper's like looking at her — I don't much want to but can't tear myself away.

Seemed harmless enough, to start. I was finding out more about the people of Red Hill than I'd gleaned in the eight years I been here — who wore padded bras and long-line girdles, who went without underpants, who was going to what party, who'd wear expensive dresses once and then try to return them the next day, smelling, Delphine said, of cigarette smoke, perfume, and sweat.

But it didn't stop there. Before long, she's passing on nastiness about the people down at the store. According to her, for instance, isn't a soul works there doesn't steal. "Joe Clyde got him a belt, two pair a Gold Cups and some English Leather today," she whispers. "Must be stocking up for Christmas. They'll all start now."

Next day, she confirms her own rumor. "What'd I tell you, Miss Mattie — Tara Hartnett's purse was so full she couldn't get it shut today. Saw her cram three or four packs of hose and some jewelry in there myself."

Holidays are the peak times, she says, and summer, when the high-school and college kids come to work. "Doesn't take them long to get the lay of the land," she tells me. "Soon's they see how it is, they want their part of the action, too." High-school kids are the worst, Delphine says, lacking the judgment to be discreet.

"Know that little snit Carolanne Morris?" Delphine's whisper weaves in and out of my days like the steady hiss of a radiator. I do know Carolanne, her momma sings second soprano at our church. Carolanne's a cheerleader at the high school, one of those tall, slim blondes Red Hill seems to spit out one after another. Delphine says, "One day last summer she walked out of here wearing three designer bathing suits, a slip, four belts, and a couple of push-up brassieres." Her voice gets thick with happiness when she tells this stuff. "Walked right by *him*," meaning Ham, of course. "I like to died laughing," and over the wires came a choking, muffled sound, like she might still.

It was around then that I started having a little trouble with Delphine's calls. I mean, here's Jimmy Lee coming home complaining about Ham and his daddy putting the burden on him of solving the shoplifting problem down at the store, fussing about how come he always gets the dirty jobs, about having to watch for suspicious-looking people and maybe having to install some kind of anti-theft system. And here's me with the best poker face I can muster, fixing supper, pouring ice tea, listening to a familiar whispering in my head while I do dishes.

But I didn't say anything to Delphine. In fact, I hardly ever talk when she calls. I'm just a listener, somebody for her to tell what she knows, which is a lot. Hidden way back in that dressing room like she is and being naturally quiet and still—keep from calling attention to her face, most likely—Delphine not only has opportunities to know most everything about everybody at Turner's, but half the rest of the town, too. It's shocking, what all goes on in a dressing room.

Take the gossip she picks up when women customers go in there together, for one thing. "It's like I'm a piece of store furniture," she says, bitter little voice rasping through the wires. "They'll say anything in front of me." It's probably more like those women been avoiding looking at Delphine so long that by now they forgot she's there, which I don't tell her. No point in it. But, anyhow, that's how we first got wind of Stella Haygood and Ham.

Stella's been working at Turner's for about a year now, ever since she and her husband Hay split up and he left her with those two boys to care for. She wears skirts so short Delphine swears you can see her privates. "No underwear, either," she tells me, "just panty hose, high heels, and them skirts." Whenever she goes to the stock room, according to Delphine, every man in the place hangs around back there, hoping for a glimpse of her bending over or reaching up high. She doesn't mention Jimmy Lee by name, but then she doesn't have to. I can see him doing it, right along with the rest of them.

"Thing I can't believe is, it's been going on right under our noses!" Delphine was purely indignant. "And if I hadn't overheard Lucile Brooks filling Sally Thomas in on the details of how they been sneaking around together for the past couple months, no telling when we would of found out." Made her mad as fire just to think of it. Delphine prides herself on being a fountain of knowledge.

I wasn't all that surprised. Ham strikes me as just the kind of man who'd have affairs with a woman like Stella Haygood. She's about as different from his stuck-up wife Celeste as I am, and not in much of a position to quibble. But the truth is, I'd rather not know for sure. Which it's too late for now. So whenever Jimmy Lee'd come home bragging on some wonderful idea Ham came up with or telling what a smart businessman he is, it's all I could do not to flat out ask him does he think it's smart business to be fooling with the help.

All things considered, I was getting more and more uncomfortable with Delphine's calls. Couldn't tell you exactly when she started referring to me and her as "us," but that's part of what I didn't care for. Plus that Miss Mattie business, and finding out more than I wanted to know.

"I got to go now, Delphine," I say, trying to be polite, and her just talking right around it, weaving her whispers into my head. Voice gets a little peevish, is the only way I can tell she hears. Sometimes I think she makes things up, trying to keep me hooked.

Wish I thought the story she told last week was made up.

After closing last Thursday, Delphine said, she went to Winn-Dixie to get her week's shopping done. She always goes on Thursdays, she says. They get the meat in then. Anyhow, she gets there, fixes to go in, realizes she doesn't have her wallet, and figures she left it down at the store.

"I have a key, you know, Miss Mattie. Always have had. Mr. Turner trusts me." Delphine maintains she's the only one down there doesn't steal, and she prides herself on that. Course, she hadn't got much else. Besides, what good would a closet full of clothes do her?

"Wasn't a car in the lot, so I just park and go on in the back door, same as usual." Delphine's building up to it, I can tell by the way her voice gets. "Dark in there, and I'm fixing to turn the light on when I hear it."

Hear what, Delphine? I'm dying to say, but been listening to her long enough to know she tells things in her own good time.

"Somebody's in there," Delphine whispers, "rooting around in my office." What she calls her office is a space barely big enough for that stool she sits on all day long, and I have trouble imagining anybody rooting around in there much. But I'm too interested to interrupt, even if I'd a mind to.

"I hear whispering, too," Delphine says, "so I slip into one of the dressing rooms." And in my mind's eye I see her doing it, quick and quiet as smoke, blending her maimed self into shadows, disappearing into thin air.

Doesn't take her but a minute more, she says, to realize that she's overhearing two people on the verge of what she calls intimacy, and that one of them's Stella Haygood.

"Oh, Claude," Delphine hears her say and figures she's calling Ham by his real name, making him feel important. Next second he answers her back, cries out her name in a high, wild voice. Delphine says she felt faint then, felt the sweat break out and wet her blouse as she crouched in the dark of that dressing room, nothing but one thin curtain between her and the truth. I'm hanging on my side of the wire with my own dread sweat, waiting to hear. "It wasn't Ham at all," she breathes to me, and I hold my breath, hands tingling and numb, any number of possibilities running through my mind. "It was his daddy. It was Mr. Turner himself."

My mind went blank then, and I let my breath out all in a rush. Even Delphine was speechless for a minute. Then I heard her catch back something sounded like a sob. "Right in my office," she whispered, "I can't hardly go in there now without feeling . . . *unclean*."

I went and laid down on my bed for the rest of the afternoon, had a sick headache, which I don't usually, although my daddy was prone to them from time to time, as was his momma before him.

Very next day Jimmy Lee comes home early, stomping into the house, slamming the back door so hard I nearly jumped out of my skin. I wasn't on the telephone, though it had rung two different times that morning. I was ironing his undershorts instead, which I do on account of the fact that my maid Belle either won't or can't do them the way he likes. Anyhow, I sometimes find ironing relaxing, the rhythm of it, and the satisfaction of smoothing the cloth out.

So there I stand ironing and here he comes flying by, eyes streaming, face red enough to bust, not changing words, just flinging himself down the hall and into our bedroom where he stayed more than an hour, sometimes beating the wall with his fists or his feet, talking to himself in a terrible low voice which occasionally gets loud enough for me to hear him cursing his daddy every whichway.

Not knowing what to do, I kept on ironing till I finished and then sat in our living room still as I could. Phone rang once, about four times, which I didn't answer it. Don't know if he did or not, couldn't tell from in there. About five o'clock he busted back out, looking like a person'd been wrestling bears, mumbled something about not being home for dinner, and lit out again.

Half-hour later, the phone rings. Delphine, of course. Even more breathless than usual.

"Whoo-ee," she whispers, "it has hit the fan now, hadn't it?"

"Um hmm," I say, because she seems to think I know and I need to, since how can I figure what to do if I don't? She doesn't offer anything right off, though.

"What you been up to anyway, Miss Mattie? I been calling." Her whisper gives me shivers, and I can't think what to say.

"Ironing," I whisper.

There's a silence while she considers that. But she lets it go, I can almost hear her deciding to, and then she tells every bit of it, all in a whispered rush I gather into myself and hold, trying to remember it so I can sort through later.

Started that morning, she says, before the store opened. She was in back, scrubbing down her office and trying her best, she says, not to think of what went on in there. "Disgusting," she whispers, and I can see her, peering into dark corners and under the counter to see can she find a stray hair or some other evidence to put in her pocket and take home.

"Then I hear voices in the front part," she tells me, "at first low, then higher. Then here *she* comes, back to my place, sniveling and blowing." Delphine stayed in her shadows, she says, watching.

"In a minute, he comes too, talking in a low, mean voice, saying: 'I said five minutes, Stella. Five minutes to get your stuff and get the hell out, before I throw you out.'

"'I'm going, Ham Turner.' Her voice was steadier than I would of figured. 'But you're not through with me, not by a long shot.'"

They exchanged a few more choice expressions, according to Delphine, then Stella left.

"Wellsir, Miss Mattie, I hadn't recovered from that, when here come Mr. Turner, roaring into the back where Mr. Ham was, hadn't moved since she walked out. Mr. Jimmy Lee's right on his heels, and the store starting to fill up, it being payday and all."

I could see it, those three Turner men squaring off, Delphine in her shadows, watching, maybe whispering to herself how she'd tell it.

"'What in the hell you think you're doing, boy?' And I swear I believe people on the street could of heard him. Mr. Ham, he stands his ground, putting his hands on his hips and setting his jaw, face starting to pink up how it will.''

And what is Jimmy Lee doing, Delphine? I want to know, so I can picture the whole thing. But I have to wait—there are rules here, and I could lose it all if I forget myself.

"'You don't haul off and fire people for no good reason. Don't you know that? Where's your mind, boy?'

"Mr. Ham says nothing, just glares, eyes red and hateful as anything, then says it, quiet and low, 'Where's yours, Daddy?'

"For a minute or so after that, there's a silence so thick I can smell it. You can practically hear everybody out there in the store quit breathing, leaning over far as they dare to see can they catch every word." And I can see Delphine herself, mouth gaped open, maybe panting a little, stroking her face to beat the band.

"Then Mr. Turner, he goes at it. Yelling at Mr. Ham, that poor girl's got two little boys to feed, don't he know the state labor people'll be crawling all over them, is he stupid or just plain ignorant? All the time his voice hammering louder and louder, Mr. Ham's face redder and redder, till I thought one of them'd bust or go dumb. And standing there next to his brother is Mr. Jimmy Lee, jerking up and down to the sound of his daddy's voice like a puppet on a haywire string. I could see something was going to happen, something had to."

By now I can see it, too, clear as if I'd been there, father and son facing off about things neither one of them can own up to; Jimmy Lee bobbing, pale and sweaty and scared; Delphine's eyes glinting out from shadows; customers turned stone-still, listening. I see the truth in it—something had to happen. And whatever it was sent my husband home in the middle of the day to beat the walls and curse the man who got him.

"And just about then, when you knew it couldn't go any further without coming to blows, Mr. Turner screams out one more time about how you can't go firing people without cause, Mr. Ham never having said but the one thing, and now Mr. Jimmy Lee busts out, voice about twice as high as usual, slicing through his Daddy's roar: 'There *was* cause, Daddy. Ham had to do it. She's making trouble down here.' He waited a second, gathering himself, then comes out with it. 'She's common, Daddy, no better than a common whore!'

"Second he got the word out of his mouth, his daddy's hand shot across that little bit of space between them and slapped his face. Not all that hard—just loud, loud as the crack of a whip. And the quiet got so thick you could hear sweat fall."

I could feel it, almost like I'd got it myself, the kind of slap you'd give a kid doesn't know when to keep his mouth shut, hurting more than a fist smashing into your face, which would at least be one grown man changing blows with another.

"Worst of it was, he had to go out, back through all those people in the store, who started bustling around like they had more to do than could get done. Mr. Turner and Mr. Ham, they just stared at each other a while, then went on about their business, too. Whole store's been buzzing about it all day, people coming back here to my place, whispering and guessing.

"What'd he say when he came home, anyway, Miss Mattie? Did he tell about it? Could you still see the handprint?"

First time Delphine'd ever asked me to tell something back, and it made me see how far the whole thing had gone. I mumbled something—"Gotta go," maybe—hanging up on the whisper quick, before it could smoke itself out the phone and stay my hand.

Didn't I vow right then and there to be done with Delphine Moses?—and feel relief flood through me like a cleansing stream.

Would've, too, but how long can you go without answering the phone? Been almost a week, and things getting back to normal, though Jimmy Lee never let on about the goings-on down at the store. I wasn't even thinking about Delphine when the phone rang yesterday, not till I got it up to my ear.

"Is he there? Did he get home yet?" That whisper comes quiet as poison, arranging itself inside my head like it'd been there all along.

I don't say a word, like maybe she won't know I'm here if I just keep quiet.

"Miss Mattie?"

Still I say nothing, wondering if I hang up real soft will she know, or will she hold on, whispering out my name for hours into an empty line.

"I can hear you breathing, Miss Mattie."

I quit, but it's too late.

"Miss Mattie?"

"Um hmm," I say, and feel myself fall back into place like a dreamer into sleep.

She's satisfied now, it doesn't take much. "Mr. Jimmy Lee left the store hours ago. But I reckon you know all about it by now, eh?"

"Mmm," I say. Which is enough. I hadn't seen Jimmy Lee, and she probably knows that, but I know she's got nobody else to tell. And it matters all the world to her, how she doles it out.

"How'd he take this one, Miss Mattie?" She asks it like a person with a right to know. I draw my breath in hard and feel cold all over. A shaking sets up in my middle.

"Bet he's sorry to of stood up for Mr. Ham now, don't you reckon?"

I say nothing, and in a minute, Delphine presses on. "Breaks your heart, how those two do him."

Then she says it, whispers rising and falling. Sing-song, like she's telling a poem, or reciting legends. That's how it falls in my head, tracing words over patterns I know without knowing. Telling how that morning, when Jimmy Lee came in, Ham and his daddy were waiting. Just got the figures in on last month's inventory and they're short a lot of merchandise, something like three or four thousand dollars' worth. And didn't we give you this problem to take care of, Jimmy Lee? And isn't it just getting worse by the day? Can't you do anything right, Jimmy Lee?

"The three of them're back here — it's where they always come to talk — and it started out quiet, but you know how Mr. Turner gets. The more he worked himself up, the louder he got, till by the last he's yelling it, and everybody in the store listening, like before." In the pause before she continues, I hear Delphine lick her lips.

"And every one of them probably looking at the next, wondering who got too greedy.

"Mr. Jimmy Lee, he's looking up at his daddy, with a shine to his face like you get just before the sweat pops out. Twice he says, 'But, Daddy,' and doesn't get any further on account of Mr. Turner cuts him short, hollering louder all the time, face redder and redder, till Mr. Jimmy Lee looks over at his brother one quick time, who's standing there beside his daddy, arms crossed over his chest, looking down at Mr. Jimmy Lee like he's some store worker's got to be brought in line. And then you see Mr. Jimmy Lee give it up, slump his shoulders and put his hands in his pockets, not looking up again, while his daddy's words rain down upon him, on and on.

"Looked like nothing so much as a sad little boy, it's enough to break your heart. And don't I wish there was something I could do."

By the time he finally came home last night, I'd already eaten supper and put up the dishes. He walked right by where I sat in the den watching TV, went straight on in the bedroom without a word.

Later, when I eased into my half the bed, I smelled whiskey on him and maybe something else besides. Made myself small and quiet enough to almost disappear, and sometime during the night I must of slept.

This morning when we had coffee Jimmy Lee looked shrunk up inside himself. We didn't talk, him and me, just listened to each other swallowing. Only thing he said was he's going to his momma's for lunch, and all I said back was "Um hmm."

Phone's finally stopped ringing, but don't I know it'll start up again before long. And didn't I tell her not to call again? On the other hand, maybe I didn't, maybe I only thought so. Can't tell anymore.

And all morning long I been avoiding my face in the mirror, afraid even to reach up and touch it, for fear what I might find missing.

Between the Lines

Dear Momma.

I stop right there and stare at those words, black as spiders against the pale lavender stationery I bought me down at the store last week, which it was on sale on account of the edges being faded, plus my discount, so it was dirt cheap, but it's right pretty.

While I'm staring at the words, all of a sudden they quit making sense, they're just lines on a page. In a minute, my eyes get to watering, my breath comes short, the lines swim together, and before I know it I'm bawling like a white trash baby, same as yesterday at the cemetery. Don't know what's got into me.

Not that there's anything wrong with crying, I don't think. I personally haven't done it in a long time, which is maybe how come I can't quit, having got started. Jimmy Lee says I shamed him yesterday in front of his kin, which is probably neither the first nor the last time. He won't speak to me, he's so mad, though being it was his daddy died, seem like he'd need a good cry himself, but he won't do it. Rather be mad at me. More manly, I reckon.

How are you? I am fine, myself.

Which is how I start every letter to my momma, a line that means nothing and is almost a joke, though I doubt she gets it. Not to mention it's a lie. Still, gets me started, which is so hard I can't bring myself to do it but two or three times a year or whenever I have big news, like now.

We buried Jimmy Lee's daddy Claude yesterday.

Wonder does a comma go between daddy and Claude? I don't know. It's one of the things I hate about writing, trying to figure the way to do it proper. Not that Momma's real big on grammar—writing either, for that matter. She's got those three stepkids and a husband running her, which must make it hard to find the time, judging by the number of letters she's managed to scratch out. Course, we talk on the phone from time to time—every year on my birthday and some in-between. But even then I can hear *them* in the background. Her real family, and me just a stray recollection from another lifetime, connected by one thin telephone wire and some every-once-in-a-while lines on paper.

Anyhow, to me it's hard, trying to fix in words what you can't even get a hold of in your head.

I have this feeling about Claude Turner, that he was a pretty good man inside, though he was hard on Jimmy Lee, and me and him never changed more than twenty words all told in the eight years I knew him, since me and Jimmy Lee been married. He wasn't much of a talker around his family, and even though Jimmy Lee accuses me of being one of the world's worst, at his momma's house I hardly open my mouth, except to eat, and once to say grace.

Jimmy Lee's daddy was one of those men don't have to say much for you to figure out they got a lot of power underneath. They say he's one of the most influential men in Red Hill, though he wasn't a big joiner like some. It was more like he made things happen from behind the scenes, good friends with the mayor and all the council members. Big drinker, I hear—he could handle it—and something of a womanizer, not that that's unusual. Though my daddy was anything but. Far as you could tell he never knew another woman was alive besides Momma, which at the time didn't strike me as unusual. It's just how he was.

Claude Turner was a right good-looking man, for his age, a little beefy and jowly in the face and squared-off in the body. Looked fine in his suit yesterday. Which is fitting and a good advertisement, suits being one of the top sellers down at Turner's Department Store which Jimmy Lee's daddy started with his daddy some thirty years back, which Jimmy Lee and Ham'll run now, I reckon, though it'll likely be Ham running Jimmy Lee, on account of he's the oldest and bossiest. Thinks he's strong like his daddy, but if you ask me, he's a pretty sorry imitation. Personally I think Jimmy Lee's smarter, but he thinks Ham was sent down, and if I say anything to the contrary he gets a look on his face makes me hush.

Jimmy Lee's momma's taking it pretty well.

Well, who knows if that's the truth? You can't tell by watching if Mizz T feels anything at all. She has this thin, pinched-up face that looks set in concrete. Been ghost-pale since Thursday, the day her husband left for work and never came home, turned red then blue in the face down there at the store, in the middle of demonstrating for Sam Shuler the quality of a particular suit, grabbing and clutching himself and trying to say something before he went, but not saying it, Ham and Jimmy Lee standing on while Joe Clyde McNulty got down on his hands and knees and tried to blow life back into the man who'd been putting bread on his table for eighteen years, while Sam Shuler called the ambulance, Jimmy Lee and Ham standing there doing I don't know what. I hadn't heard that part, nobody tells about that part, they just tell what everybody else was doing, so when I try to see Ham and Jimmy Lee watching their daddy die, I can't get a clear picture in my head. Were they crying and jumping around, wringing their hands? Did they get dizzy and almost faint? Did anybody scream?

Funny, how you do when people die. You might picture yourself acting a certain way, but you can't ever tell till it happens.

My momma, for instance, screamed in church the day we buried my daddy, screamed his name, whenever they started carrying the casket out. Closed her eyes, flung her head back, held out her arms and screamed, like she was a magician and that could somehow bring him back, else like an actress, and after the scene was done we'd all walk off together, arms around each other's shoulders, laughing and discussing how it went. Lay abed for three days after, me staying out of school and bringing her soup, spooning it into her mouth like she was the baby and me the momma, she holding herself and saying she lost everything in the world. And me right there, not able to get my mouth around the words to remind her of it.

It was sudden, a heart attack, they say.

Whereas it took Daddy months, didn't it, months to watch him die by inches, till his face turned into something it hurt to look at. I remember that day I stood in the doorway of your bedroom and heard him say to you, plead with you in that raspy whisper his voice got to before it quit altogether, ask you to please look at him, how you used to. Remember seeing his eyes, the only part that still looked like him at all, fixed on you like salvation within grasp, you crying and looking down at your lap, winding your fingers around and around. Never looking up, and that was all he asked. Finally he lay still, closed his eyes like it was just too tiresome to keep them open anymore.

Later that afternoon I remember the phone rang. It was your friend Lucy, and you talked a long time, gossiping about people at work. Once you even laughed quiet into the phone, covering your mouth with one hand.

Dying slow like he did, Daddy had time to say what was on his mind, like when he told me to tend to you now, you needed me, I was the only family you had. Yessir, I vowed. I could see it, me and you looking out for each other. Which of course turned out different, didn't it? But who'd of guessed you'd hook up with Mr. Jackson and be gone to Mobile within a year? Or that you'd never set foot in Red Hill again, nor open your mouth to suggest a visit?

How's the weather in Mobile? Here's it's hot and muggy as dog sweat.

You could see the sweat staining everybody's clothes yesterday. Pallbearers looked like they might keel over themselves any minute. Everybody's hair was soaked and there was steam rising around the neck of Reverend Wilkerson's robes. Bet he dropped five pounds burying Claude Turner.

I could stand to drop about fifteen myself. Yesterday I had to leave the waist of my navy blue skirt unbuttoned, which the jacket covered it up, but I still felt not quite dressed all the same. Then whenever I started crying like I did and Thurmond Sanderson thought I was going to pass out, fall right down into the hole they dug for Jimmy Lee's daddy and were lowering him into, well, Thurmond took my jacket off and then everybody could see not only the sweat stains on my blouse but also my unbuttoned skirt which by this time had unzipped itself a little and was slipped sideways on me. Probably all talking about it today, maybe discussing if I'm just letting myself go or if I'm finally going to give Jimmy Lee the babies he deserves. Which I would if I could.

When we got home yesterday, Jimmy Lee said I acted common, then went in our guest room, slammed the door behind him, and stayed in there till supper. Don't know what he was up to, but I don't think he cried because whenever I'd tiptoe up the hall and listen at the door, I never could hear a sound.

Wonder was he remembering what he screamed that afternoon last year, screamed like nobody could hear him or would ever know he said it, wishing his daddy dead and buried and gone from this world? Or maybe not, maybe he was thinking about the deep creases on either side of his daddy's mouth, seeing that sideways swagger he had to his walk, smelling the rich smell of his Sunday pipe. Or maybe he's remembering the sound Claude Turner'd make when you did something that pleased him, a deep, drawn-out hum that meant he agreed with you. Not that Jimmy Lee heard it from him much. But maybe he was thinking of it all the same. Because when some-body dies, it's those little memories we tend to hold, like the smell of fresh tobacco or the hardness of a collarbone against your cheek. Else a certain look.

Jimmy Lee came back out in time for supper. Made his favorite, pork chops with mashed potatoes, black-eyed peas, and applesauce. But we both just put food in our mouths without changing words, and since we weren't talking, I couldn't help thinking about being dead and laid in the ground with dirt on top and what happens then, so my appetite wasn't up to usual.

After supper Jimmy Lee walked out the front door without a word while I stood in the living room with my hands down by my sides, not opening my mouth or moving, not knowing was he coming back, maybe he'd go somewhere and turn blue too and never come back, that's how mad he is. Then I heard his steps and he opened the door and stuck just his head in, not looking at me, mumbled something about going to be with his momma a while. It's enough to make you ache, how some people'll choose to grieve.

Hope everything's OK with you. Write sometime and let me know.

Now I've told about the death and passed along the weather and politeness, I've got nothing left to say that I can put down on paper.

If it was Daddy I was writing this letter to instead of you, I could tell him things I wish I'd said back then. If you'd asked me to look at you, Daddy, I'd say, I would have—I always *was*. But you didn't know it because you were always looking at her. I'd tell about being married to Jimmy Lee Turner, James LeGrand Turner, I'd say—what do you think about that, Daddy? Wouldn't he be surprised? And we got this big, nice house, with lots of things in it and pretty furniture, but nothing else. I'd say, me and Jimmy Lee don't have much in common, Daddy, so it's not like it was with you and Momma.

But maybe I'm wrong, maybe we really do. Because seem like Jimmy Lee and me been spending most of our lives looking at people who're looking somewhere else. And now both our daddies're dead, so we have that in common, too. Even if he is mad at me. Even if I do shame him.

Well, I better go. Got to get this house cleaned up before Jimmy Lee comes home for lunch.

Which is a flat-out lie. It's so clean now you could take it for a museum, and what's more, Jimmy Lee's going to his momma's for lunch today, so I got all afternoon to kill. And sometimes I wish I didn't, I get so tired of inching through it.

Cut my finger fooling with the edge of my new stationery. I squeeze it and one round drop of blood comes up out of me, which I push till it falls, a perfect circle, on the faded lavender paper. And I think about sending the letter like that, not even signing my name to it, conjuring her face when she gets to that part.

Over Bridge

Jimmy Lee's been talking lately about we need to have wills drawn up. He says, and I'm sure he knows, that the state'll get half of everything unless we do. Fine, Jimmy Lee, I tell him, go ahead. Says he'll talk to Bubba McKenzie—Bubba's a lawyer here in town, Jimmy Lee's golf partner—about doing it.

So far, though, he hasn't.

I can't decide if he thinks *I'm* fixing to die or he is. Either way, I think it scares him—that anybody's going to.

After yesterday, though, and what happened at bridge club, I believe I'll tell Jimmy Lee he can do what he likes, but I'd just as soon the state get my part.

Lord, I got to get up out of bed and get this house straight. Belle comes tomorrow. She gets mad when I leave things out. Won't say a word, just sets her mouth and shoulders hard, and only half cleans.

Jimmy Lee didn't even notice I didn't pick up after bridge yesterday. That's because my club meets in the living room and Jimmy Lee never goes in there unless I ask him to change a bulb in the chandelier or something. Claims he can't breathe in there. That's how he talks. Doesn't say much, but when he does he's always exaggerating.

Anyway, *we* can breathe in there fine, especially since Tootsie quit smoking. She was the last holdout. She would be. Tootsie Middleton's always doing something they say is bad for you. She's on the wild side.

Tootsie, Ida Jean Munroe, and I have been playing bridge together going on seven years now. Thelma Sanderson started with us back four years ago, I guess. Took Jane Ann Patterson's place. Jane Ann died in childbirth—can you believe that, in this day and time?—it was so sad. But anyway, we had to have a fourth.

We were lucky to find Thelma. You got to be careful who you choose for a bridge partner. Sometimes they last longer than a husband. I was the one who found her, at the checkout in the grocery store. We were waiting in line, got to talking. She was new in town. I liked her right off. Only been here fourteen years myself. One thing led to another, I got her number, and we had coffee.

We play bridge every Wednesday afternoon, taking turns whose house we go to. Seems like Wednesday afternoon's when everybody plays something in Red

Hill. The bank and all the Front Street stores close at noon, the men play golf, and we women play bridge. You'd be hard put to find a doctor after twelve on a Wednesday, too.

Course Mac used to stay open. He was no golfer.

I know it's ugly to talk bad about the dead, and I don't mean to. There's nothing bad you could say about Mac. He loved women, is all. He and Doc Logan were the only two doctors in Red Hill worth shooting. Doc Logan's been my doctor for years. He's steady and old and dry, and I reckon he'll quit soon. He's a GP, which is what a town this size really needs. And I don't believe he even *likes* women, much less loves them.

Mac, though, was a doctor for female problems, an OB/GYN, and I guess you could say he loved his work.

Once he even got shot at for loving it. Fred Parsons, over at the bank, found out that Mac and Mary Lou, Fred's wife, had been seen together down by the river. Fred went berserk. Brought a pistol with him over to Mac's office, busted in right past Mac's nurse, Ellen Gennery, and started screaming and threatening. Gun went off two or three times, one of which times Fred shot himself clean through the foot. Mac patched the wound, Fred went on back to the bank, and it was all over but the talking it to death.

People found it hard to stay mad at Mac. I don't know exactly what was so appealing about him. He was short, ginger-haired, wiry. Looked like a young Red Buttons. Had green eyes and a one-sided smile.

Irish, I reckon, by his name: Andrew Jamison McGill. Or maybe Scottish. I could picture him in a kilt. His legs were muscular—I saw him in shorts once—and covered with a light fuzz that turned gold and red when the sun shone on it.

Not that I found him appealing in the least. Like I said, Doc Logan's my doctor. I did start to go see Mac a few years back, to find out why me and Jimmy Lee couldn't have babies after I lost that first one. Tootsie told me I should. But Jimmy Lee wouldn't let me, said it was none of Mac's business. Just as well, I reckon, the way things've turned out.

Mac supplied this town with a good portion of its scandals in the past few years. Never did get married, and he didn't much care who else in town had. At his funeral—Mac died in a car wreck about six months ago—I heard you had to get to the church a half-hour early to get a seat. Cars were parked more than three blocks away, they said.

Anyhow, the reason I'm thinking about Mac today is because of what Ida Jean Munroe did yesterday at bridge. Ida Jean's the oldest one of us four—I don't know exactly how old, but I'd guess somewhere around fifty, though I'd never say it out loud. And she's a widow, has been for fifteen years. Somebody told me her husband was so glad to get shed of her mouth, he went out with a smile on his face. And it's true that the woman can talk. Ida Jean works down at the courthouse, in the clerk's office, so she always knows whatever's going on. Loves to tell it, too.

But yesterday beat all. Yesterday Ida Jean brought to our bridge club the last will and testament of Dr. Andrew Jamison McGill.

We'd just settled into our chairs. Thelma was sitting across from me. We're partners, like Jane Ann and I used to be, and we understand each other pretty well, even without the eye twitches and under-the-table foot nudges Ida Jean and Tootsie use. I was shuffling. I like that: the sound and feel of it takes my mind off things. Sometimes when I get to feeling edgy or low, I'll get me a deck of cards and start shuffling and pretty soon I feel better.

But Ida Jean stopped me in mid-shuffle yesterday when she said, looking slyly across at Tootsie and cutting her eye at Thelma: "Y'all'll never guess what I got in here."

She patted her purse and looked wicked, the way Ida Jean does when she has big news, like that time she told about our librarian Miss Pringle running off with the girl's basketball coach. Ida Jean has kind of heavy jowls that shimmy when she smiles. It is not a lovely sight. She's one of those people who look better frowning.

We all looked at her, knowing it was something juicy. Ida Jean loves to try and spin out the suspense.

But this was too good. "It's Mac's will." She looked around at us, cheeks quivering something awful. "It just got out of probate yesterday. I made us a copy."

Lord, it got quiet in my living room. I was quiet because it was the first I knew people could get a hold of something that secret, and after you were dead too: the last words, in a way, you leave behind. Seemed like opening the casket up, peering in at the private parts, sifting through the bones.

I felt Tootsie rock back in her chair. I looked up and saw Thelma gone dead pale.

"Shitfire, Ida Jean! How in the hell'd you get that thing?" It's not unusual for Tootsie to talk like that. Like I said, she's wild. I've heard her say worse.

Now Tootsie and Ida Jean have been bridge partners these past seven years, but the truth is they're not what you'd call friends. They're about as opposite as two women can be. Tootsie's never married, though once she lived with a man, right out in the open, for about a year. He moved off. Since then Tootsie hangs around evenings down at Chuck's Diner where lots of the men in town go after work. She drinks beer with them and sometimes, they say, one of them will see her home. She holds down a good job over at the dress plant, works in the office there, takes care of herself, and, far as I'm concerned, whatever else she does is her business. I like her all right, though every year she does seem to get wilder. Truth is, I reckon she wouldn't of been playing bridge at my house this long except for the fact that we been doing it forever and she *is* a Middleton, even though she acts like she forgot it and they mostly don't claim her. Whereas Ida Jean is, as I say, a widow. She is also a Baptist.

Ida Jean smiled even wider. "I reckon parts of this thing will surprise some people," she swung her head slowly over towards Thelma, her face shaking like vanilla pudding, "and maybe not others."

"That's not legal, Ida Jean, is it?" Thelma's voice was quiet and thin. "Having that will, making a copy. You're not allowed to do that, are you?"

"Once a will's filed in the courthouse, Thelma honey, it's in what they call the public domain. Anybody can get a copy of it. Didn't you know that?"

Thelma didn't answer. Ida Jean sat back in her chair and unzipped the top of her purse, very slowly. She was having a good time.

"Well, goddam, we going to play cards here, or have court? I'm not listening to it. It's none of your goddam business, Ida Jean, nor ours either. Deal, Thelma."

Ida Jean looked at Tootsie, then narrowed her eyes. "Y'all don't have to listen to it, if you don't care to. I just thought it'd make entertaining table conversation."

Well. I was shocked, like I said, about this rummaging about in a dead man's words. But the room was thick as molasses with something I all of a sudden wanted to know about. Like a bad itch you can't help but scratch.

"We can take a minute, can't we? Is it long, Ida Jean?" I even surprised myself, saying that. Thelma was biting on the inside of her lip, how she will when she's trying to think what card to play. Tootsie's face was streaked with red, like she'd put on rouge without a mirror.

But Ida Jean was pleased enough to flash her teeth at me. "Not that long. I can skip the whole first part, where he leaves his house and all to his sister. You know, the one who lives in Texas? The interesting part is the list, anyway."

"List?" Thelma and Tootsie sounded like an unpracticed chorus.

Ida Jean smiled, said, "Um hmm," in a pleased, high voice, and opened the folded papers.

We sat there dumb as mummies while Ida Jean flipped over the first couple pages. She was humming to herself, just loud enough for us to hear. Other than that you could hear dust fall, it was so quiet.

"Here it is, here it is." Ida Jean jiggled and bared her teeth. "'I hereby give, devise, and bequeath the items described hereunder to the following persons.'"

She looked around at the three of us and grinned, teeth sparkling like knives.

"It's alphabetical."

There was a sharp intake of breath from either Thelma or Tootsie, I didn't know which, and I couldn't take my eyes off Ida Jean's awful mouth to check.

"'To Sarah Lynn Anderson, my Cross pen-and-pencil set.'" Ida Jean paused to let that sink in. Sarah Lynn is E. D. Mooney's assistant down at the drugstore. She's a plain-faced woman of around forty-five or so, Tommy Anderson's wife, nobody I'd ever thought much about before.

Ida Jean continued: "'To Josephine Buchanan, my Turkish bath towel; to Lucy Carmichael, my tongue depressor; to Marilyn Cuttino, my red cashmere cardigan; to Geraldine Edmonds,'" Ida Jean paused and licked those loose lips of hers, "'my cordless Swedish massager.'"

Ida Jean sank back, taking a little breather on that one. I was picturing that prissy Geraldine Edmonds in church, sitting next to her thin-lipped husband Farley, and trying to make sense of it all when Tootsie stood up suddenly, waving one hand and knocking over the dish of mints by her place.

"Ida Jean Munroe, this is the limit! I'm not sitting here another minute listening to you read that man's private words."

Tootsie leaned across the table towards Ida Jean. Her voice got quiet. Her mouth twisted like she was fixing to spit. "You sad, old, dried-up bitch."

She straightened, looked at me and Thelma. "I'm through with this. Been through really, just didn't know it till now." She pushed her chair under the table, raised her chin up high. "Under the *M*'s, you'll find Mac left me his red plaid bathrobe, as I'm sure you already know, Ida Jean. He left me that because I used to wear it after we made love. Know what that's like, Ida Jean? Want me to tell you the things we used to do together? How he made me feel good? He was a doctor, you know. He *knew* things. Want me to draw you pictures, Ida Jean? Maybe you could try some of it out on yourself."

After the front door closed, Ida Jean broke up and started sniveling. I looked over at Thelma. She was ashy and wouldn't look up, so I went to the kitchen to make coffee. By the time I got back, Ida Jean had composed herself and Thelma had gone to the bathroom.

Ida Jean said she reckoned she'd go on home since it didn't seem like we were going to get any bridge played today. She was slumped and old-looking when she got up. I told her bye and didn't see her to the door, just sat there looking at the folded-over papers she'd left on the table.

Seem like my hand had a mind of its own, reached itself out and picked those papers up. My eyes scanned the names, three-and-a-half pages of them. Mostly women I know, of course. Items ranging from his stethoscope and rubber gloves to his blue silk pajamas and clock radio. Left Mary Lou Parsons his twenty-two.

I had just turned to the last page when I heard Thelma. Looked up and saw her, white as the door-frame she was leaning against. Then I looked down and saw her name, right after Peggy Reardon's: "To Thelma Renee Sanderson, my gold monogrammed cuff links." Funny, I didn't even know her middle name till then.

Thelma walked over to where I was sitting, took the will out of my hands, and stared down at the paper. She ran one finger across the words written there. She said: "He couldn't have known anybody'd be able to get this."

She smoothed the paper again and put it back on the table, then crossed her arms and looked down at me. "Ah, God," she said, and her eyes filled, "what in this world am I going to do?"

I figured she meant about Thurmond, her husband, and their little boy, Robert. For a minute, looking at Thelma's face all fallen in like that, I wanted to get up and hug her, help her figure something out. Then it came to me, maybe that wasn't it at all. Maybe she was thinking about Mac instead, how she missed him.

Either way, seemed a little late to start worrying now. She should've had Doc Logan for her doctor. Like me.

"Know what I think, Thelma?" I smiled, sparkling my teeth up at her, and started clearing the table. "I believe that's just a list of Mac's patients, don't you reckon? He wanted to leave them all a little something. That's what I think. That's what anybody'd think."

Thelma didn't say a word, just looked at me. I could feel my smile hanging crooked on my face. I kept my eyes shiny and friendly, humming a little under my breath while I cleaned up. She said she had to go.

At the door, Thelma turned and started to say something, then thought better of it. Just as well.

Don't know what we'll do about bridge club now. Start over, I reckon. I'll call Ida Jean later on, see what she's got to say. And when Jimmy Lee comes home for lunch today, I'm going to break it to him about the state getting my part. Don't worry, Jimmy Lee, I'll say. Maybe you'll get lucky and die first.

Seeing Things

Thought I saw Bobby McAllister yesterday, right on the street. Well, across it. It was the walk that stopped me cold: head high, cocked a little to one side how he did, arms swinging wide. Could have been the hall of my high school, thirteen years back. It was enough to make the hairs on your neck prickle.

After he passed, I sat on the bench outside Mooney's Drugstore and stared across at the vacant lot they're fixing to make into a park. I was there so long Sarah Lynn Anderson came out the store to see about me. Was I all right, she wanted to know. I said yes. Got up to walk off and fell down flat, right on the Front Street sidewalk.

By today everybody'll know about it, probably say I've taken to daytime drinking. Probably say, yes, I thought so, she always was a strange one. Clucking tongues and shaking heads like they're getting bad news they been expecting for years.

Jimmy Lee'll hear for sure, down at the store. Somebody'll be dying to tell it. People love that, don't they? He'll come home for lunch, ask me how come I didn't tell him and what's the matter with me anyway. He'll say I should go see Doc Logan. Fainting means female problems, heard him tell his brother Ham that once when Celeste was having spells. Like he knows the first thing about female problems.

Anyhow, I'm not going. No reason to. What I fainted for they can't cure.

I can close my eyes right now, lying here in my unmade bed at ten o'clock on a May Monday morning, and see my whole life, like it would've been if I'd of waited on Bobby McAllister instead of marrying Jimmy Lee.

First thing I see is me walking next to Bobby, my arm tucked under his. We're smiling, going somewhere. We have things to do, I don't know what. Just things, that we do together. He's happy I'm with him. I'm having to take quick steps, keep up with that long stride of his. Not that I mind. I remember the muscles of his legs showing clear through those light khaki work pants he used to wear. Only saw him in shorts once. I stared and stared at his knees, wanted to put my mouth on them in the worst way. Never will forget the sweetness of the way his calf muscle curved.

We'd of had a big family, me and Bobby, probably three or four kids, some boys, some girls, and our own little place, maybe down in Baytown, with shutters and a yard. He'd keep it painted nice, and I'd plant flower borders everywhere and cook big suppers and work down at the church whenever I liked. Of course we'd have a dog and a cat, and maybe even some hamsters. I hate the nasty little things, but in this pretend life even they seem cute, and our kids are crazy about them. We watch TV together on Saturday nights after the kids go to bed and hold hands like we're kids ourselves and laugh and try to keep each other quiet so we don't wake them up. You know how hard they are to get back down. Sometimes he picks me up and twirls me around, bends me backwards, surprises me, just for the sheer pleasure of it. My hair is long and I'm slim and pretty, even after those five or six babies, and when he twirls me I laugh and laugh till he has to kiss me to get me to hush. Then I kiss him back and he picks me up, wherever we happen to be. I don't know where the kids are during this part, but they're never around. He takes me into our bedroom and makes love to me, starting down at my toes, which he loves, he actually loves my toes, and then working his way up, just like this man in a book Tootsie Middleton gave me to read. And I'm humming with that old, sweet, rising-up feeling, and he is, and we are.

I'd never daydeam about Bobby getting hurt down at the store, something falling on him maybe, and him mutilated something awful and then dying, leaving me to figure how to spend the insurance money. It's shameful, but sometimes, when I hear an ambulance go by, I imagine that, picture Jimmy Lee being put on the stretcher, never coming through the door of our house again.

Used to play this game, after Bobby left, and me and Jimmy Lee got married. Still do, sometimes. Goes like this. I'll be doing my regular household things: buying groceries, cooking supper, or just walking around the house trying to figure what to do next, and then I'll pretend Bobby's looking out of my eyes, seeing what I see. And the game is, he doesn't know whose eyes he's inside. He has to guess from what he can see. I don't ever walk past a mirror when I'm playing, see, because then the game would be over, even though sometimes I'm tempted to, to see what he thinks of how I look now. I don't though. So he has to figure out from the clues he can see, the different things I do in my day, whose eyes it is he's seeing through.

Used to be a lot of fun. I could put Bobby in there behind my eyes and keep him in suspense for hours. I don't know where I go myself, when he's inside. Just off, somewhere quiet. Then Bobby'll walk around in my house, mine and Jimmy Lee's, doing my chores, trying to figure out who I am. Sometimes it's embarrassing, like when I go to the bathroom. I wonder what he's thinking then. Makes me feel funny.

Course the game's automatically over the minute Jimmy Lee walks in. I always try to get back in before, but sometimes I don't pay close enough attention. When Bobby sees Jimmy Lee, he gets angry and sad, says to let him out, not to call him back again. So I don't play it like I used to, though sometimes now seem like I go away and there's nobody left inside at all. Which is scary, when I come back. Like going into a haunted house by yourself.

Besides Bobby's knees and the curve of his legs, it was his mouth that appealed to me most. It was one of those mouths that doesn't have definite edges, the lips are just part of the face, kind of like that French actor Jean-Paul Belmondo, but nicer. So whenever Bobby kissed, it was like his whole self was doing it, not just lips. He kissed for the sake of it, he loved it that much. Not like Jimmy Lee, who acts like kissing is a formality you got to start with when you want to get down to business. When I close my eyes and concentrate, I can still feel the gliding, silky smoothness of the skin inside Bobby's lips.

What keeps bothering me is this: how come he didn't look over, yesterday, on the street, that man walking, looking for all the world like Bobby McAllister? Couldn't he feel me looking at him? If he'd just turned his head. Sometimes just a turn of the head can make all the difference. Just a little thing like that.

To be fair, when I finish thinking about how my life might of been, I try to give Jimmy Lee's other life a look too, the one he'd of had if I'd waited on Bobby. I just have to relax my eyelids and let it come.

Jimmy Lee would of married somebody like my sister-in-law Celeste. Probably Sally Parsons, else Charlotte Worthy. One of those girls born knowing who she is and what she's supposed to be doing at all times. Blonde. One his momma could've liked, maybe. Jimmy Lee and Sally/Charlotte would've had two perfect little children, a boy and a girl, one named for his daddy, the other for his momma, with middle names from Sally/Charlotte's family, and cute nicknames like Trey or Doodle. Sally/Charlotte would be a perfect size 8 and a good party-giver. She'd probably model clothes for the store sometimes, with their two blond-headed kids. When she talks, Sally/Charlotte chooses just the right words. She thinks Jimmy Lee's momma is sweet and his brother Ham is a kind man and a business whiz. She and Celeste shop together, their hair pulled back by black grosgrain ribbons into little blonde ponytails, their feet in espadrilles, both of them walking that duck walk that gives them away a mile off. At lunch they sip white wine and talk about their friends, which they have a million. They dress their children alike, too. She has this house looking like something out of *Better Homes and Gardens*, though she never cleans it herself, especially not before Belle comes; and Belle respects her, says, yes ma'am, Mizz Turner, and looks down, the way Jimmy Lee's momma's maid does.

How's that for happy endings? We'd both of got what we needed if only I hadn't said one yes to Jimmy Lee Turner's asking me out all those years ago. One word, one time, one thing, and everything changes. If I hadn't, I'd of been a regular wife, the kind of woman who has babies and keeps them, who likes having sex with her husband, the kind whose female organs act proper and do their job instead of all the time hurting and bleeding out their misery.

If I hadn't, I wouldn't be lying here in my bed thinking about a man I hadn't seen nor heard from in thirteen years, waiting on my husband to come home for lunch and fuss at me because I fell flat on my face in the street yesterday, wondering am I going to lie here and listen and hold my mouth still, or will I open it and let words pour out, scream out what Thelma Sanderson told me when she called yesterday morning, about my husband Jimmy Lee Turner and Miss Marianne Luquire, that sweet-faced young woman who teaches Sunday school at our church and serves on the membership committee Jimmy Lee's the chairman of, that's been having so many long meetings this past year, how Thelma's husband Thurmond heard from Tom Emory that he saw the two of them having dinner last Saturday night at Pittypat's Porch in Atlanta, Georgia, where Jimmy Lee happened to have been, gone for the weekend to a buyer's convention.

If I hadn't said yes all that time ago, I wouldn't be lying here in my bed feeling my woman-blood soak these sheets and wondering to myself am I crazy, or have I dreamed it, or is it true Bobby McAllister's been dead these past eight years, wondering can I really see that newspaper notice like it was in front of me, reading Robert M. McAllister, Jr., fell from the seventeenth floor of a building he was working on in Dallas, Texas, fell down and down and down again, never knowing what hit him, never turning to look, never seeing that beam swinging long and low towards the back of his head.

Getting Through

"It's up to us to make this work, Mat. It means a lot to Ham." Like I care. Of all the arguments Jimmy Lee could've conjured to convince me, seem like he'd of known that's as sorry as they come.

Maybe he did, too, because the next thing out of his mouth was, "Think of Momma, Mat." And me saying to myself, strike two, Jimmy Lee.

But I reckon I am thinking of her some today, plus the rest of those Turners, as I put up gifts and throw out wrapping paper, save bows and store boxes, trying to put one more Christmas behind me.

Yesterday marked my fifteenth Christmas at Mizz T's, which is what I call Jimmy Lee's momma in my head, though to her face I've always said Mrs. Turner, which seems more fitting. Ham's wife Celeste calls her Mother Turner, but then she would. Anyhow, she's got kids and I reckon that makes some difference.

This Christmas looked to be different, what with Ham and Celeste separated and maybe getting a divorce and Ham's having that little girlfriend and all. I was curious to see what we'd do, but I knew Jimmy Lee'd get around to telling me whenever he thought I needed to know. So when he came home for lunch one day last week, informing me we're going through with everything as usual, like nothing's changed, I reckon I wasn't all that surprised.

Mizz T's been sick this past year, angina's been acting up something awful, so Ham didn't want to trouble her about him and Celeste. Said he thought her heart might not could take it. And Mizz T doesn't get out much any more, so she hadn't heard it yet. No pun intended, and by that I mean she's so hard of hearing that for her to have heard it, somebody'd have to yell it or write her a note, one.

Personally, I think Ham's more worried about the fussing he'll have to take from his momma than any taxing the news might put on her heart. But who knows.

The puzzlement to me was how Ham'd talked Celeste into going along. She's one of those women who seem to have been put on this earth for the express purpose of making the rest of us realize how God intended us to look. Hair's honey blonde—her real color, probably—straight, thick, and shiny. Wears it in a smooth pageboy which she sometimes pulls back into a low ponytail fastened with a flat bow. She's had two kids, but you can't tell it at all from her figure, and her face is smooth as a baby's. I always thought maybe she didn't have wrinkles because she doesn't change expression much, and maybe that's right, or maybe I'm just being ugly because my figure looks like I had babies even though I haven't yet and because my face has a few lines. But still. It's true Celeste doesn't smile much, nor frown either, for that matter. Her eyes are cold blue and never rest on you, just flicker down and then away real quick, like she couldn't be bothered to look long. To call her stuck up is so mild it's almost a lie.

She's so icy and far off even Mizz T's nose twitch can't get to her. She either doesn't see it or else it just wouldn't occur to her to take it personally.

Mizz T has this unfortunate facial tic, where her nose goes to one side and she sniffs and closes her eyes. It looks like she smells something so bad she can hardly stay in the room with it. Seems to be specially afflicted with it when I'm around. Once I started to ask her did I smell bad, but then I didn't because Jimmy Lee's momma is not exactly blessed with a sense of humor. She does laugh every once in a while, but it's a dry clack way in the back part of her throat. Sounds more like choking. Not enough practice, I reckon.

Strangest Christmas we ever had, before yesterday, was the one after Jimmy Lee's daddy died. Celeste's and Ham's kids were little that Christmas. Margaret was ten and C3 was eight, and I guess they missed their granddaddy. Not that he ever played with them or even talked much. He'd get himself settled in with the paper or football on TV and every once in a while he'd offer up some comment or ask was dinner ready. But he smoked a nice-smelling pipe, and that, mixed with the smell of his favorite wool sweater and his red leather chair, was somehow a comfort, even to me. If Mizz T missed him, you couldn't tell it, except that her nose, which is thin and pinched-looking anyway, seemed thinner than ever and white as bone around the nostrils.

Every Christmas since, Ham's been trying his best to take his daddy's place. Carves the turkey, sits at the head of the table, wears a wool sweater, and watches a lot of football. Stops short of smoking a pipe, but I bet he's considered it.

Course, Ham was his daddy's favorite, his name-sake: Claudius Hamilton Turner, Jr. His momma calls him Claude Junior or just Junior. The rest of us call him Ham. Always seemed fitting too, because with his tight collars buttoned up to where the loose skin of his neck almost gets caught in them and his bright pink-complected face, he looks to me like nothing so much as a dressed-up porker, a shoo-in for the blue ribbon. He was a star football player in high school, and I think he played some in college too, but that bigness has turned on him now. And I guess he can't help his name, but did he have to go and name *his* son the same thing? I always wondered that. Course they call him C3, meaning Claudius the Third, like some Roman emperor or English king, which was OK until that *Star Wars* picture came out and it sounded like he was named for a space robot.

Mizz T won out when it came time to name Jimmy Lee, though. She'd lost a baby in between, a little girl, carried full term and then born dead, got twisted inside her and strangled herself trying to get out. So two years later, when she had him, he was plain old James LeGrande Turner. Nothing Latin, just family names. Seemed like to me Mr. and Mizz Turner ran out of steam by the time they got to Jimmy Lee. She was thirty-six then, a year older than I am now, and Jimmy Lee was her last, and she knew it. He's always been her boy.

Yesterday started off promising. It was clear and cold and fresh. Jimmy Lee lit the fire soon as we got there, and Ham and Celeste and the kids came in right after, along with Margaret's boyfriend from college, Hank somebody. He and Margaret generated enough electricity to about light the room, acted like they were the only people there, or wished they were. And looking at the two of them made me feel sad all of a sudden, for no good reason. I got up and went to the bathroom a while, just to be by myself. Which I do a lot when we go to Mizz T's house anyhow.

When I came back into the living room a few minutes later, the scene was like something off a greeting card. A perfect Christmas morning: fire sparkling, Jimmy Lee sitting next to his momma on the sofa looking at her new cookbook, which was one of the items we gave her—she doesn't use them anymore, but she likes to collect them—Margaret and Hank sitting on the floor fire-gazing, C3 putting together his new microscope—boy's a science whiz, they say, making straight *A*'s in chemistry this year—and Ham and Celeste, standing over near the lighted Christmas tree, looking for all the world like two people who'd been happily married for twenty years. Christmas music was playing, a little loud for my taste on account of Mizz T's hearing, but pretty all the same. And though I knew it was silly, my eyes filled up and I got a terrible lump in my throat. Like I couldn't tell what was real from what was greeting card. By the time the room came back into focus and I got hold of myself, it was time for us women to go get dinner ready. Mizz T'd done a lot ahead of time and we'd all brought something, but it had to be put together. You know.

So Celeste and Mizz T and I went into the kitchen and started heating up and stirring and ladling into other dishes. Can't serve anything from the stove at Mizz T's. Not on Christmas, not ever.

Mizz T and Celeste talked about this and that, Margaret's boyfriend and what sorority she got into and if C3's going to go to college like he wants or if he's going to work in the store like his daddy wants. Celeste was even more reserved than usual, which is not surprising. I don't ever talk much around the two of them because I feel like they're waiting for me to make a mistake, which I always do. Besides, once I get started I have a hard time stopping. So I mostly just listen.

Yesterday, hearing Celeste talk about Margaret, I picked up a wistful something in her voice. Struck me all of a sudden that Celeste's college days had probably been her high point. She'd been queen of the May and head cheerleader and all. Now here she was twenty years later married to a man who's making a fool of himself over some little red-headed slip of a girl half his age, a clerk down at the store, and everybody in town knowing it.

We put dinner on the table, called the men and kids in and said grace. They let Margaret's boyfriend do that since he was new: it was a good way to test him out. Which test I myself failed miserably some years back when it was my turn, mumbling God is great — the only blessing I knew — then eating the first thing I could grab, which turned out to be stuffed celery. My chewing made such a commotion even Mizz T heard it. It was my first and last invitation to say grace, and to my knowledge they never again served celery at that table.

But Hank did a nice job, didn't use an already made-up one, just said to bless us all for being together on this special family occasion. Which struck me funny, considering, till I realized that's just what it looked like. Even I couldn't tell the difference between Ham and Celeste that day and any other, back when they were living together.

Just then the phone rings. Margaret's closest, and you know how teenagers got to go hellbent for the phone. Seem like they always think it's for them, no matter whose house they're in. So she dashes for the phone, which is in the little hall between the living room and the dining room. We all get still and hear her voice, quiet and cold, saying, "Yes, he is, he's eating his Christmas dinner."

There's a pause before she heads back into the room, her face pale. Lord, didn't she look like Mizz T just then, and I'd never seen that before.

"Daddy, it's for you," she says, lowering herself into her chair like she thinks she might break.

Ham's face goes even brighter pink than usual, and he almost tips his chair over backwards when he stands up. Mizz T, at the other end of the table, goes on eating and doesn't raise her head, so I can't tell if she even knows the phone rang.

Now, dinner at Mizz T's is generally quiet as a empty house. Nobody says much, and you can hear the clink of the silverware, the rumble of stomachs, and the wind blowing outside, if it happens to be. I try to chew real quiet, after that celery episode, but you can always hear yourself swallow. You just hope nobody else can.

But yesterday, after the ringing of the phone and Ham leaving the table, there's a stronger kind of silence, deep enough to hear heartbeats. Celeste is sitting across from me, and I actually see hers, pulsing at the side of her neck so hard looks like it's trying to get out. I meet her eyes and she meets mine at the same moment we hear Ham whisper something low and urgent out there in the hall.

That look of hers rocked my foundations. She loved him. Good Lord. Who'd of guessed Celeste could feel that strong about anything, much less Ham Turner? But it was clear she did, and it answered my question about how he'd gotten her to go through with this.

In my side vision I glimpse Mizz T, alone at the head of the table, slowly lifting a forkful of turkey to her mouth, face like a mask. I see her thin hand tremble.

There's only the one phone at Mizz T's, right there in the hall, and I suddenly realize we're going to have to make noise or listen, one. Still looking at Celeste, I open my mouth. Nothing comes out. Again I try—it's like priming a pump. This time, the words come a gusher.

"Mizz Turner," I holler, taking into consideration her affliction, "I do dearly love your asparagus casserole; Lord, what *would* Christmas dinner be without it?" On account of my being nervous, my voice may be even louder than I intend. Mizz T's head jerks up like she's been shot, and her mouth comes open, but she doesn't answer fast enough; here comes Ham's voice again for a second. "Hank, honey," I yell and he jumps in his seat, "don't you just love this asparagus? Have you ever in your life tasted anything so good?" Could he guess, I challenged him, what all's in it? But before he can answer—I swear seem like everybody's in slow motion and I know I can't let the noise stop and for some reason all I can think to talk about is that stupid asparagus casserole—I go on; like I said, once I get started there's sometimes just no stopping. So then I holler to Celeste does she know how to make it. "I myself never got the recipe from Mizz T." I say that right out, Mizz T, first time I ever did, but I'm in a hurry; I see her face flicker, though her tic doesn't kick in. But Celeste doesn't answer either, just blinks in surprise, and I'm getting ready to educate Margaret as to the quality of this particular asparagus when C3's steady little scientist voice interrupts with: "Asparagus, boiled eggs, bread crumbs for topping, and a cream sauce made with milk, flour, and butter."

Everybody's looking at C3 then, and just as he finishes saying *butter,* we hear a final whisper from the hall and then the receiver being quietly hung back up.

Ham doesn't come right back. We all hear him go into the powder room there in the hall, hear him peeing, then the toilet flushing. You can hear everything through the walls in Mizz T's house. She doesn't know it, though. Which is just as well.

Jimmy Lee clears his throat when Ham comes in. I can't bring myself to look at him or say another word. I'm plumb winded.

Then Mizz T turns to me, says she never heard me call her Mizz T before. She rather likes it, she says, and smiles at me in a kind way that makes her face look almost pretty. At which time I'm really winded.

We ate. I don't know how we got through it, but we did. Give you an idea how strange it was though, nobody said a word to C3 when he finished dinner, brought his microscope to the table and starting inspecting the leftover food on his plate. Watching him do that, I got to wondering what you'd see if you looked at us through one of those. Reckon you'd see blood and bones and muscle and skin. But what else would you see when you looked inside me? Or if you looked into Mizz T, would you find that young woman who bore her daughter dead into this world and was left with two sons like Ham and Jimmy Lee? Could it show you where Celeste's ice came from?

We cleared the table, took the dishes into the kitchen and started serving up dessert. Standing there with the two of those women, smelling the spice of the pumpkin and the richness of the mince and maybe a little of our sweat because the kitchen was warm, and some of our womanness mixed in together, standing there cutting pie and listening to the hiss of the teapot and the perking of the coffee, I saw how much alike we were, Mizz T, Celeste, and me. I'd never thought that before. It's funny that yesterday, a day when the family was coming apart, I felt for the first time that I had a part in it.

As we carried the pies out, Celeste looked me full in the eye and said, "Thank you." And while she might of meant for holding the swinging door back for her, I don't think so.

Whenever we left, Ham and Celeste were standing next to Mizz T, waving good-bye to us. I don't know what'll happen to them. Maybe they'll get back together.

Today I stared in the mirror for ages, trying to see could I catch a glimpse of who I used to be, or even who I am now. I'm wondering about Jimmy Lee and me, about do we get along OK or are we a greeting-card marriage. Is everybody, maybe? I try to think am I happy or not.

You know what? I believe I'm going to pack up the rest of these Christmas decorations today, even the tree. When Jimmy Lee comes home for lunch, he'll be mad as all getout because he likes for them to stay up until after the Epiphany. Some Episcopalian custom or something. But this year I want to start the new year off clean.

Lord, I'm all of a sudden tired of this Christmas clutter.

Due Dates

"Waiting more than she then we then," the one nurse says to the other, who nods like it makes perfect sense, turns her head towards the first one and moves her mouth. I can see it yawing up and down, but I don't hear this one's words at all, which doesn't seem to trouble that first one, who laughs and asks, "We can go can you can go can?" You can tell it's a question by how her voice goes up at the end.

"Please," I whisper. "Talk sense." I feel my lips shape the words but I can't hear. Inside my head feels like cotton's been stuffed far down into my ears, which feeling I recognize from having tried that remedy to cure myself of waking to Jimmy Lee's snoring, which it doesn't work, but I've tried unlikelier things. Anyhow, that's what this feels like.

Those two're ignoring me, looking at some chart

up there on the wall. And here I lie on a bed in the hall like something half dead, or at the very least deaf as a doorknob. Hey, I want to holler, but I can't even whisper. Look at me, here behind you. I'm alive, I'm a woman, I'm one of you.

I mostly like it, too—being a woman. That penis envy thing Jimmy Lee told me about when we were arguing one time is plain silly. Somebody made that up, is what I think, and a bunch of people swallowed it. I mean, maybe when you're in the woods and you got to go, it'd be a right nice thing to have, a convenience. Otherwise, it'd just be in the way all the time. It is anyhow, even not attached. It'd look plumb ridiculous in a tight skirt, or short shorts, or panty hose. Then, too, every time you feel sexy or something, people know. I think that's a big drawback. Also, and I'm not too sure on this one, but I think crossing your legs'd be uncomfortable. I know *they* do it, but it must kind of mash it. Anyway, like I said, mostly I'm glad to be a woman.

Never told any of that to a living soul. Jimmy Lee'd die if he knew I even thought about such things. Truth is, it's only lately they been on my mind. And ever since they gave me that shot a while back, to relax me, they said, and help me rest, my mind's been going every whichway.

Lord, don't you hate hospitals? This one was just updated and they keep talking about how proud they are of it, how modern it is and all. I've only been in here once before, but I swear I can't tell a bit of difference. Walls still that sick minty green. Somebody must've told them it was a color that'd make people hurry up and get well so they could get out quicker. That's all I can come up with. And the smells. It's a bunch of bad ones mixed together with something like Pine Sol thrown over the top. Hate to think what all these smells are, but I just can't help it. They're everything that comes out of us: pee, sweat, blood; I don't know what all else. Fear, that has a smell. Death. Reckon they can't make a disinfectant strong enough to cover it.

Wish I wouldn't think about this stuff.

Never much minded how blood smells, though, really. Kind of rich, with a tang to it. Coppery, I read that somewhere. Seems right, too.

I remember when I started my period. It was early, I was only about ten. I was proud, once I got over being scared to death. At first of course I thought I was dying because Momma hadn't troubled to tell me about it, me being that young. So I thought I was dying, and in a way I guess that was partly true. The girls my age were kind of awestruck. Envious, too. We sang a song about first comes love, then comes marriage, then comes somebody with a baby carriage. Momma said that could really happen now. I could have a baby. Shows how much she knew.

Seemed like magic to me, the blood coming, once a month, like a full moon. Still does. Even when it hurts, even when it won't quit.

Jimmy Lee'll be here after while. He isn't coming till it's over. Probably haul some flowers up here with him. Else candy. The thing to do. His momma might come too, do her duty. She's big on that.

Hardly anybody else knows I'm in here. Not that I'm ashamed or anything. Just didn't come up in conversation, you know? Jimmy Lee always says I have a big mouth, and I reckon maybe I do sometimes, but I just didn't feel much like telling this.

Lord, I've had the strangest dreams lately. Usually I can't remember. They say you dream every night, but I don't believe it because, if so, how come I can't remember? But these I do. Can't put them out of my head.

It's two different kinds of dreams I'm having. The first ones are about me: I see myself without arms or legs, or missing a breast or part of my face. In one of them, and I can't explain exactly how it is, but I'm nothing, just nothing. I'm trying to look in the mirror and see myself, but I can't, because I'm not there. That one's got me waking with the cold sweats.

Rest of the time, I dream about babies. Not sweet, healthy ones, like Celeste's were, or like the ones my momma used to keep, back so many years ago I can hardly picture it. My dream babies are sick, deformed, terrible. Babies who have scales instead of skin, or no arms, or one foot where the belly button's supposed to go. One-eyed babies. Awful twisted hurt babies, one right after the other. Babies that can't survive. Makes me so sick and scared, I wake up choking, can't catch my breath. Bad enough having to dream them, but then they won't go away. Pop into my head all day, taking me by surprise like a child trying to scare its momma by jumping out from around the corner and shouting boo.

Nearly dozed off, I reckon, but now I open my eyes and the lights are too bright so I squint and there's somebody else with those nurses now, too. A black man, young, all dressed in white and in a second he turns around and smiles and leans down closer to my face and says "You're chicken," or something like that, which I resent, but still he *is* smiling and for all I know he's right, so I let it go and then his face disappears and I close my eyes again.

Only other time I ever remember dreaming about babies was when I was pregnant. Lord, must be what, fourteen or fifteen years ago. But those dreams were sweet. With my eyes closed like this, I can still see the little light-haired boy who used to come to my dreams then. Never saw his face, but I knew he was mine, the one I was entrusted to carry, keep safe inside me till he could gather up enough strength to make it on his own. I'd dream him walking down the road with a fishing pole, barefooted, mouth pursed to whistle. Or sitting at a little desk, reading, the light shining on his white-blond head. Aside from the hair color, he bore a strong resemblance to my daddy.

I remember waking up smiling, putting my hands on my belly to try and feel him in there. I swear he did move once, even though Doc Logan said that was impossible, I wasn't far enough along. Still. I thought so, and it was my body. He was my baby. What did Doc Logan know?

I remember the morning I woke up crampy, like I was getting ready to start or something. When I went to the bathroom, I found that spot of bright redness on my underpants, and in my head came a noise like sirens. Seem like I just stared at that spot the longest time before I could think what to do—one of those times when your mind goes blank, says to you: stop. Maybe it was an hour I stared at it, maybe just a minute, I don't know.

Doc Logan put me to bed and said don't move unless you have to. For two weeks I did that, didn't move, lay there and tried to hold my baby in. But it didn't matter. Because the blood just kept coming, seeping out at first, then in clumps and pieces. For the life of me, I couldn't connect what was happening with my dreams. Which had by that time quit altogether.

Then came the day I was alone in my bed, concentrating on holding in but tired of it all the same, when a terrible wave of cramps hit and I went bent over with them to the bathroom and passed something, I don't know what because I couldn't look, I just couldn't. Then I flushed the toilet and went back to bed and when Jimmy Lee came in that evening I told him I thought I'd lost the baby—said it right out like that, but it didn't seem real to me. Jimmy Lee called Doc Logan and he came over. I'd just woken up when he got there, and the cramps had eased some.

Doc Logan was trying to be nice about the whole thing, I guess, but he seemed to take it pretty lightly.

Comes into the bedroom and says to me, "What happened, Mattie?" I tell him best I can. Then he looks me square in the face and asks me this: "Did you save it?"

Inside my head his question explodes into tiny pieces, piercing jagged edges everywhere. I am filled with red pain and I can't help it, I open my mouth and scream at him.

"Save it?" I holler. "Did I save it?" Doc Logan's jaw drops open and he moves a couple paces back from the bed. Which only makes me madder. I want to fling myself from this bed, cover the distance between us with one leap and beat my fists bloody against his chest and face.

But all of a sudden I stop cold because I feel something shift in my heart, and I know past doubt that this's nothing I can blame on Doc Logan. It's my fault, plain and simple. And the knowing knocks me dumb, and I break down and cry. Which I wish I hadn't, in front of him.

After while, Doc Logan uses his driest voice on me, explaining that what he meant was, did I save the fetus, the thing I had passed and was afraid to look at. "No," I whisper, thinking and trying not to of how in this world I would've done that. No. And Jimmy Lee standing at the door, looking scared and alone as me.

Week later Doc Logan put me in the hospital and did a DNC because I couldn't get rid of the pieces that were left inside. It's like my body was holding on to those last little bits. That was when I was in here before, in the maternity ward then, too, with this same awful color on the walls.

Kind of pitched a fit when I found out they were putting me on this floor. Seem like a mean joke. Kept at Jimmy Lee till he finally got Doc Logan on the phone, but Doc Logan told him to tell me that's the way it was always done, for me to calm myself down, it was the only room available. So yesterday I lay in my bed waiting for today, listening to babies crying and mommas hushing them.

A shivering has set up inside me now and I squint over where the nurses were but nobody's there anymore. Seem like I'm shaking my covers and this bed and maybe the walls too, my teeth setting up a clickety-clack rhythm I can hear through this cotton they put in my head. Then into view comes that young black man in white again and I feel something warm as bath water cover my body and he's smiling and murmuring while he tucks a blanket in around me. Hot tears fill my eyes because I want to say thank you but my lips won't move. Then he's gone again, so I might have imagined him, but now I'm warmer.

Reckon Doc Logan'll be here directly. Not that he's doing it himself, just that he told Jimmy Lee he wanted to see the job was done right. The job — how's that for matter-of-fact? Course, maybe doctors have to be. I remember him telling us after my DNC that he didn't think I'd be having any children, there was too much scar tissue in there, he'd never seen so much, it was a miracle I ever got pregnant in the first place. When I close my eyes and try to picture inside myself, I see walls like a cave's, covered with thick, raised, dark-red worms. I want to ask: where did they come from, those scars, am I cut up inside? I want to, but I don't. Doc Logan's voice is so dry, seem like words turn to dust before they get out his mouth good. Besides, I'm afraid what he might answer.

And isn't it funny, how things work out. Because I always thought I'd have me a house full of babies. Been dreaming of that since I can remember. Figured it was one way you got to be a woman. Which seem like I've spent most of my life trying to do.

Course, Jimmy Lee and I've had some good dogs. Four of them. Two got run over, one just disappeared, and we still have our collie, Sam. And I sure have loved them, but it's not exactly the same, is it? None of them ever reminded me of my daddy, for instance, or my momma, who I hadn't laid eyes on for going on seventeen years, who doesn't even know I'm in here. I couldn't figure how to say the words on the phone, much less put them on paper. And anyhow, what good would it do? Just give her one more opportunity to tell me she's doing the best she can, but she does have her hands full, what with that family of hers, and if there's anything I ever need, just let her know.

Still, I reckon Jimmy Lee and I've had it pretty good, overall. On account of his family owning Turner's, I get all the clothes I want, just about, even though they're generally last season's. Towels, too, china, casserole dishes. They carry Corning, which I love, specially that new flower pattern. I play cards a

good bit, mostly solitaire anymore, plus I enjoy a
good jigsaw puzzle. And I am learning to grow things
in my garden, which makes me feel good in a way I
can't explain. Jimmy Lee has his golf, his card games,
and his brother Ham to look up to and complain
about, plus we got this nice four-bedroom house
overlooking the third tee of the only golf course in
Red Hill. I'm not sure what else you could hope for.
Course every now and again, I still miss that little
house we started out in, over in Baytown, the one
where we lived next to Thomas and Celia, where I
lost the baby.

Know what I think about sometimes? Somewhere
in that yard lies that baby boy I used to dream.
Because I didn't know enough to save him, he's back
there. Before we moved, I bought me a big can of
wildflower seeds, sowed them all over that backyard,
hoping to make his grave pretty. Used to drive by a
lot, but the flowers never did come up, so I quit. Last
time I looked, there was a swing set back there,
which is better than nothing.

Being moved now, but my eyelids are too heavy to
pry open. The air against my face is cool and I hear
the squeak of the wheels this bed moves on.

Lord knows one thing—I'm clean enough to
meet my maker. Between the shaving, the enema,
and the douche, they took care of my insides, plus a
hair-washing and a shower for the rest. Even made
me take off my toenail polish. Feel like I'm fixing
to be embalmed or something. Purified with for-
maldehyde.

Whenever Doc Logan told me I was going to have this operation, that I needed to let them take my uterus out because of the bleeding and that scar tissue, he acted surprised to death when I started to cry. I couldn't have babies anyway, he said in his gritty old voice, and this'd make me feel better. It was the sensible thing to do. What was my problem?

"Wonder will I still be a woman?" I asked Doc Logan that. Didn't intend to — he's probably the last person in the world could figure what I meant by it — but it just up and came out of my mouth like somebody else's question. Seemed to take him back some. Don't reckon he was ever asked that before, ever thought it even. Didn't answer me, either, just went shuffling off, mumbling under his breath, kicking up a dust trail as he went.

Now I hear voices and they're messing with me, sliding me off this bed onto something else and I'm cold again right off, my teeth chattering and the light very bright, right through my eyelids glaring and I hear a sound that seems familiar but I can't focus on it. Hear voices, too, though not words, just "waw waw waw," in a fog, in a cloud, but that noise underneath and steady and then I all of a sudden do know that sound: it's my heart, speaking out for all to hear, it's my heart, and even as I listen it picks up pace.

Tootsie

Tootsie left town yesterday. "Before I get rode out on a rail," she said, looking sideways at me, raising those penciled-in brows high up into her red bangs as they'd go, eyes wide and funny, saying, "Course, you never know, might be fun, eh?" Then laughing that deep chuckle in her throat, the one I've tried to copy and can't.

That's one of Tootsie's best things, how she's just about always laughing, no matter what.

Tootsie Middleton lays claim to one of the best names and worst reputations in this town. I sat next to her at bridge for seven years' worth of Wednesdays without getting the first glimmer of the kind of woman she was. Then we had that nasty breakup where Tootsie quit in a huff, Thelma Sanderson left town with a short, red-headed encyclopedia sales-man, and Ida Jean Monroe developed a chronic shake to where she couldn't hardly hold cards in her hand. I have since given up bridge for solitaire, which is better in a lot of ways, because you don't have to clean house, serve food, or even get out of bed if you don't care to.

Anyhow, figured I'd seen the last of Tootsie Middleton that time, and didn't much care one way or the other. Didn't know enough to. This time though, I feel like a part's been cut right out of my middle. "Buck up, sweetie." She'd say that to me now. "Don't let 'em see you down." "'Em" is what Tootsie calls everybody she doesn't consider "us." How I got to the plus side of her system is a mystery I'm beholden to.

What she looks like is a floozy, sort of. Wears the highest high heels I ever saw on a white woman. Windblown-looking hair that's redder than it used to be, plum-shadowed eyes, fingernails sharpened up out to here, pale, thin skin and high cheek color made higher with that Revlon cream blush called "Autumn Splendors." Looks like she has a fever sometimes, what my momma used to call hectic spots. Acts that way, too, like a woman burning up with it, saying anything she pleases, doing what she wants. Always did, especially after it was understood that the rest of the Middletons had disowned her, beginning with her own momma and daddy, who washed their hands way back when she first dropped out of high school and started working to earn her living instead of going to college and marrying well like everybody always planned, and including even her cousin Celia, who didn't do all that hot herself, by Middleton standards. This was before my time, but I know all about it. Have to be deaf, dumb, and blind not to in this town. People talk about that stuff like it just happened yesterday and still matters.

"A teacher. Ha. Can you picture me a teacher? Or anybody's wife?" She asked me that, the time she was telling about it all, putting the pieces together for herself, with me just there for the comfort of a face to look at from time to time. I think she needed to see me to know she was here and now, to keep from getting lost in the back-then. Course, I *could* picture her a teacher. That's what she was, though not the kind she meant, maybe.

Tootsie came to see me in the hospital, two days after they relieved me of my womb. Only visitors I'd had up to then were Jimmy Lee and Mizz T, although Lucile Sweeney had called to tell about how she felt after her hysterectomy, and Mary Kate Culhane sent a long note detailing the positioning of her sorely tilted uterus and telling how any day now, she was going to have to have the same thing done, or worse. Said she had to sit and stand a certain way to keep the whole shooting match from falling right out. That wasn't something I knew about Mary Kate, barely knew her at all, really. But I was coming to see that certain circumstances make women tell things they wouldn't normally, and a hysterectomy is one of them. My close-mouthed maid Belle Besselieu, for instance, described to me her sister-in-law's "hysto-my-rectomy" from start to finish, including her waking up in the middle of it to find her uterus half out and the doctor and nurses taking a coffee break and telling jokes. Later, Belle said, they told her she was dreaming, and maybe she was. Even Mizz T confided in me, telling about that girl baby she bore dead, in between having Ham and Jimmy Lee. Didn't look in my eyes while she talked, but I saw pain in the thinning of her lips.

Tootsie breezed in that ugly little hospital room at ten in the morning. Visiting hours didn't start till two, but I could see why nobody'd stop her, in her tall, pale, snakeskin shoes and big-shouldered jacket. First thing out of her mouth was, "Why in the name of God are you on the maternity ward?" Looked at my face, hugged me, said "That goddam Doc Logan. Don't get me started on him," then proceeded to start. Made me laugh by telling about the time she went to his office because she'd got the itch. Told her problem quietly to Doc's nurse, Megan Donnelly, who's even older than Doc and can't hear worth shooting and won't wear her aid. Miss Donnelly clucked in sympathy, wrote down "cramps." Tootsie repeated her problem a little louder, moving her lips slower, too. Miss Donnelly smiled and nodded, pointing to the word she'd written. After the second time, Tootsie gave it up, hollered to the nurse and the twenty-some ears perked up behind in the waiting room: "Crabs, Megan. Little, itchy, sideways-walking critters that like dark, wet places. Crabs." Then sat to wait for her ointment, staring down any pair of eyes that dared to venture up. That was her last visit there.

Tootsie said Doc Logan's basic philosophy about a woman's ailments is, "If it ain't in her head, it must be in her vagina." Said I was lucky he didn't do a lobotomy for good measure, where they take out the part of your brain that makes you feel. I was thinking to myself maybe they did.

Told her the question I asked Doc Logan, about being a woman, after. Just kidding, I said. But Tootsie's eyes filled. She came to where I lay propped up in the bed, sat by me, held my head against her breast, and rocked with me back and forth until I couldn't stand it anymore, that holding. Just then we heard, in the distance, in the halls, the babies. She said this to me: "You don't know it now, and you may not believe me, but you're going to be all right. This is an end, no question about it, but it's a beginning, too. Don't forget that, sweetie. It's your beginning." After while, I hushed crying, she left, and I slept. That was how we started, and she was right, about the beginning part.

I'm not the only one who thinks so. Jimmy Lee traces things back to then, too. Says I *changed*. Says it in a suspicious way, like I changed *into* something.

I don't know if he ever found out Tootsie'd been to the room. When I woke up next day, I wondered for a while if I'd dreamed it, a visit from a fairy godmother. Because I felt changed somehow. Inside me was a lightness, in a place that'd been heavy so long I'd quit feeling the weight. In a way it was my womb, and the old dreams I kept so long. They were gone. But instead ·of feeling dead, I just felt light. That night I had a dream of being so light I rose up and floated, like a party balloon, or a ghost. Maybe that's what being dead is about, a lightness and a leavetaking. I don't know.

What happened next was that Tootsie started coming over to visit. That first evening she dropped by after work, Jimmy Lee and I'd just finished supper. She knocked once, opened the screen door, and came in, shouting, "Anybody home?" Jimmy Lee jumped up from the table like he was going for his gun, a man defending his homestead.

Tootsie waltzed in wearing red high heels and a red suit that somehow didn't clash with her hair, though all the magazines say it will. She eyed the supper dishes, saying, "James LeGrand Turner, I trust you didn't let your wife fix this, she's not well enough yet," which of course I had, but neither of us said a word. She put her arm around me, lifted me out of my chair, said we'd go sit on the porch while Jimmy Lee took care of the dishes. Which he did, without changing words. We could hear the water running from out there.

"I'm going to take you in hand, sweetie," she told me that night as we sat on the porch swing, smelling wild rose and honeysuckle and listening to Jimmy Lee do dishes. "As my project. I need one, and you're it."

She laughed and leaned her head back against the swing.

"You and me, we're exact opposites, I been thinking that. I was born in and been trying to get out all my life, where you been out so long you don't even see what you're looking in at anymore."

When Tootsie left that night and I went inside, Jimmy Lee was sitting in front of the TV, playing with the remote control.

"What in hell does *she* want?" he asked me, in between punching buttons. I looked at him, not answering. He kept flicking channels. Seemed so like a little boy to me, I had the urge to go over and pat him, tell him it would be all right. But looking at the set of his shoulders, I went to bed instead.

Tootsie was good as her word. Took me to the new mall on the bypass to shop for clothes, showed me how to do three-layered eyeshadow, taught me gin rummy and spit, made me laugh, talked to me. In all my thirty-six years, nobody ever talked to me like that. Except me, to myself, which doesn't count.

Hadn't been out the house so much in ages. At first, it made me dizzy. I was scared, wanted to quit, go back where I'd been. But Tootsie was hard to turn down. I was her project. And dizzy started feeling good to me.

The day Jimmy Lee came home from work to find me dressed in a hot-pink jumpsuit with my nails fresh polished and my hair styled off to one side, he stood in the doorway like a man waiting to be shot. He rocked back on his heels, wet his lips, said, "Mat?"

"No," I said, smooth and cool as silk. "Matilda."

That was maybe the best thing Tootsie gave me— my name back. All my life people called me one thing and another. Momma called me Sister, why I don't know. With Daddy it was Tillie, people at school called me Mattie, Jimmy Lee and his kin said Mat, or "her." Then Tootsie named me Matilda. Said it was royal, a queen's name. I saw I'd never called myself anything before. Now I did. Matilda. It made all the difference.

Funny, how Tootsie gave me that, taught me lessons she couldn't learn herself. Because all the while she was bringing me out of where I'd been, she was sinking deeper into a mess herself. Which I didn't know at the time. I had all I could do just putting one foot in front of the other. But it wasn't any different than what Tootsie'd been doing for years.

Courtney Elizabeth Middleton gave herself the name Tootsie when she was in high school. She picked it, she claimed, because it was the trashiest she could think of, the one she hoped her momma and daddy would hate most. Maybe it was the same reason she picked Jake Remedes for a lover, not her first, because Tootsie started young, but the first one that counted, because everybody found out.

Jake was a smooth-talking engineer the dress plant imported all the way from Atlanta to fix one of their machines. Tootsie was a fast rising junior at Red Hill High, had an ID card that claimed she was twenty-one. "And the body to back it up," she told me. This was about two weeks ago. We were sitting on my porch. Jimmy Lee'd gone to play cards down at the store, and Tootsie was settled in for storytelling. What she started out with was sex, which somehow brought her around to the subject of Jake.

"Lord, he was handsome. Exotic, with all that dark hair, those flat-planed cheeks. Had these goddam hot, black eyes that'd flick up and down your body till the heat'd make your knees wobble. Liquid eyes. I'd never dreamed of a man like that, Till."

Having christened me Matilda, Tootsie had taken to calling me Till. Said it fit, that I was just here till I took my life up and got on with it.

"Course, I hadn't had a taste of anything but boys, up to then." Tootsie laughed and rolled her eyes at me. "Which ain't all bad, either."

I knew Tootsie'd been fooling around with Johnny Ryan, a high-school boy who works down at Mooney's after school. She hadn't told me, but I knew. Everybody did. I was hoping she'd have the sense to quit before she got herself in too deep.

"By the time Jake found out I was sixteen, he'd already invested too much time and effort in me to let go. Besides, he'd taught me so well, he'd addicted himself in the process. Before school, at lunch break or recess, after school, nights, mornings, weekends, in his car, or mine, or a stranger's, on the dirt, grass, carpet, floorboard, in motels, under stars, in broad daylight. Anywhere, anytime, every way you can think of, and more." Tootsie groaned and leaned back against the swing, stretching her body out against her purple velour running suit.

I couldn't think of but two ways, and I have to admit hearing her talk like that made me nervous enough to chew the inside of my lip.

Tootsie took a deep breath, let it out slow. "Besides all that, Till, Jake made me laugh. I don't know what about. Just that when I look back at it, all I can remember is making love, and laughing. Never could resist that in a man.

"He was going to leave his wife, of course. She was having a baby, but I didn't know that till later." Her voice took on that hard edge it sometimes gets when she talks about men.

Tootsie pushed herself up out the swing and started pacing my porch. Seem like she forgot me altogether.

"When I hadn't had a period in two months, I went to Dr. Taylor, over in Salters Corners. You probably never heard of him—before your time—but that's where a nice girl who thought she was in trouble went, back then. He was the unofficial county abortionist. An old man, an old office, an old tradition of getting unpleasantness out the way with the least possible fuss. Had to park around the block because everybody'd automatically know what you were there for if you parked at Dr. Taylor's. People'd make a special trip by there just to check out the cars. After while, even going to Salters Corners was enough. Wasn't any other reason to be there.

"I went, peed in a jar. Few days later, he called, told me I was going to be a momma. If I wanted."

Tootsie stopped talking but kept pacing. I was thinking about a sixteen-year-old Courtney Elizabeth Middleton, going by herself to pee in a jar and wait for news. Thinking how funny life turns out. Picturing

Jake Remedes's hot, black eyes inside a red-haired baby's face.

"Called Jake at his motel. We met down by the railroad tracks, in a little shanty we used sometimes. I never will forget his face, when I told him. It was the strangest mix of feelings, each one struggling with the other. And I swear to God, Till, one of them was *pride."*

She stopped short, spit like a man into the azaleas by the porch, whispered, bitter as seeds, "Bastard."

Tootsie dropped back down on the swing, looked at the ceiling. "That's when he told me Maria was pregnant, too. He couldn't leave her. I was too young, he was old enough to be my uncle." She snorted, shook her head. "He said that—my uncle.

"Then 'Uncle' Jake looked sideways at me through those silky, black lashes, said, 'Anyhow, how we supposed to know it's mine?'

"At first, I wanted to hurt him. Pick up a two-by-four and smash his beautiful face with it, till there'd be nothing left but pulp. Then, while I looked at him, inside me something changed. I got up and left Jake Remedes, propped on one elbow, eyes glinting with something I half understood and couldn't bear to see.

"Next day, I cut school, drove to Salters Corners, parked at the drugstore, walked to Dr. Taylor's, lay myself down on a little table in his back room, and opened my legs for him.

"'Count backwards,' he said, leaning over me. I could count the furrows in his forehead, his spiky nose hairs. He moved then. I smelled a sharpness and started at a hundred. My tongue swelled inside my mouth. The dots on his white-tiled ceiling dimmed at ninety-six, disappeared by ninety-three.

"Woke up in a dark room, lying on the examining table, under a sheet. Freezing. Teeth-chattering, knee-knocking cold. I could see my clothes, folded neatly on a stool, out of reach. It was dark, quiet, cold. I called out, or tried to, but my voice was broken, hoarse, like I'd been screaming. It occurred to me that Dr. Taylor'd gone home, left me there alone, for the night. Or that I was dead, just not gone yet. But I was too cold for that."

Telling it, Tootsie's voice went hoarse. Her teeth began to knock. I watched a hard shiver go across her, there on my porch swing.

"I got up to get my things, get warm. Stood and felt something, looked down to see a bright, bright red-ness flowing like a spring stream, warming my legs and making my head go light, and knowing I was going to fall, and then doing it, falling and falling into space, like in a dream, falling."

It was quiet enough on my porch to hear the two of us breathing and the chirrup of a cricket who lacked the grace to be still. I was seeing blood, feeling a dream-fall.

Tootsie sat up. "Dr. Taylor had to call Doc Logan to stitch my eye where I busted it, and to make the other things right. Seems problems weren't all that uncommon with Dr. Taylor's 'procedures.' That's what Doc Logan called it, a 'procedure.'"

Touching the end of her left eyebrow with one finger, Tootsie turned, seeing me for the first time in ages, saying, "Can't hardly see it anymore, sweetie. I pencil right over it." Smiling at me, like either of us believed that was enough.

"I didn't want Jake anymore, but I brooded so over it, almost went crazy. Went to school, but nothing would sink in. I was continually cold. Couldn't stand it. And of course, people talked. Nothing concrete, just a certain look, and a smile. You know how they do.

"Finally decided there was only one way to make it better. Wrote a short, mean note to Mrs. Jake Remedes, over in Atlanta, and mailed it off.

"A week later she showed up. At school. It was sixth period, I was coming out of study hall, and here's this pretty, little, dark woman, hardly looked older than me, belly pushing out against her dress. Dark eyes, like Jake's. She put her hand on my arm, said, 'You are Courtney Middleton?'

"I knew who she was. I nodded. The halls were full of people changing classes, but I remember feeling like it was only the two of us standing there. Some kind of vacuum closed in around us. Couldn't keep my eyes off hers, could see clear to the bottom of them. I knew in that moment that I had done a terrible thing.

"Not taking her eyes away, she brought herself closer to my face, said, 'I am Maria Remedes,' then began a high-pitched keening, teeth together, mouth set somewhere between a smile and a grimace. It started out thin, then she took a breath—so close I could feel the heat on my face—and turned it up. It was sound without melody, grief music. Still holding my arm with her hand and my eyes with hers, she pitched that noise higher. And louder.

"My hair stood on end, my eyes ran water, my ears ached. Still higher she went, and louder, till my knees gave way and I fell to the floor, holding my empty belly and screaming for her to stop. When she did, finally, it was worse, that silence full of the sound that had gone before.

"Then she said it in words, quietly, not wiping the tears that fell down her cheeks like spring streams, fell down and wet me as she stood over me, telling it, what I'd done to her, telling it there in the hall with every student and teacher at Red Hill High hanging by, mouths agape.

"She finished, reached down, lifted me up, helped me to the steps outside, brushed her hand lightly over my ugly black stitches, and walked away."

Tootsie left the swing and sat herself down on the steps. The outline of her face against the porch light was sharp enough to draw blood.

"That was my last day at school. Two days later I moved out of the Middleton house." It was the first time Tootsie'd ever talked to me about her parents. Her voice was young and bitter.

"Daddy wanted to 'sue the bastard.' Always thinking of the money angle. Momma wanted as little to do with the whole thing as possible. Tried to send me to St. Mary's, bury me in a convent.

"So I left. Got a job at the dress plant, through a man I met once with Jake."

She turned to me, grinned. "Became the Tootsie you have come to know and love."

Her face softened into something like it must have looked twenty-five years ago. Her voice was soft, too.

"I'm not sorry for any of it, really, Till. Except the one thing, hurting that woman who never hurt me. I'd take that back, if I could."

She pulled her knees up to her chest and hugged them against herself for warmth, shivering still. I stepped inside, pulled the afghan off the sofa, put it around Tootsie's shoulders, and sat next to her on the steps. She leaned her head on my shoulder. I put my arm around her. I could smell her hair spray.

"Goddammit, Till. It was so frigging long ago, and you think you're past it, but it never goes away, does it?" She didn't care if I answered, so I didn't. We looked at the stars. I could make out the two dippers, which is all I ever learned, anyway.

"Guess you heard I been seeing Johnny Ryan, huh, Till?"

"Um hmm," me trying to keep my voice even.

She was quiet such a long time, I thought she was going to leave it lay. Then, "I know it's wrong, Till. But I can't help it. He's so goddam sweet. Thinks he loves me. Sometimes he wraps those strong, young legs all the way around me, calls out my name, and I want to cry with it, his sweetness. Can you understand that?"

I pretty well could, and said so. Tootsie seemed happy with that. After while, she went on home, and

I didn't see her again till she came by yesterday, to tell me she was leaving.

"Charleston, Till. Where I should have been all along. Big enough to be myself in. Got a job lined up, and an apartment. Soon as I get settled, I'll call you to come spend a few days. We'll do the town up right."

I was squatted in the dirt, planting a spring garden I could hardly wait to see blossom. As I looked up at Tootsie, dressed in turquoise and pink, red hair glinting in the yellow sun, cheeks and eyes and fingers and toes colored bright as jewels, she suddenly seemed like a miracle to me. I lost my breath, looking up.

Bird of paradise, I thought. Not even clear what one is, if it's a real bird, or a flower, or what. It just came into my head. Bird of paradise.

"Close your mouth, Till, before a bug lights in it." She laughed and pulled me up. We sat on my porch steps like we had two weeks before. Only this time, there was something different in her, a softness taking up some of the hard places.

She kissed me goodbye, right on the lips, and said we'd keep in touch. When she left, I went inside and lay on my bed, stared at the ceiling, like I used to do for hours. It doesn't work anymore, though. Can't get away from myself like I used to. So after while I went back to my planting. In the evening, Jimmy Lee came home, we ate supper, watched TV, and went to bed.

And didn't I dream young John Ryan's pale, Irish eyes inside a red-haired baby's face.

Seeds

—————————◆—————————

"You're going to get worms, doing that." That's what Jimmy Lee says every time he catches me biting the dirt out from under my fingernails. To myself I think—uh uh, Jimmy Lee, it's the other way around, eventually. But I keep quiet on account of that's the kind of observation gets on his nerves something awful.

Got plenty of the stuff under my nails this morning. Which makes Jimmy Lee say he feels like he's married to a farm worker, though even he can't deny how good the yard's looking.

To me this dirt tastes bitter with a clean undertaste, which I reckon is a kind of funny contradiction, but true. And I could probably lie here on my bed half the day cleaning myself and trying not to think about yesterday, but eventually what I'm trying not to think about would push itself through, so I reckon I best get going.

My friend Charlie Simpson says dirty fingernails are the surest sign of a serious gardener. When I went down to his store the other day to get some plant food and a few other things, Charlie said I looked like a little girl in my overalls. Said I was the cutest thing he'd seen all day. Mildred Pyncheon heard him, too. He didn't lower his voice or anything, and I saw her eyes flick up and down at me like I was wearing hot pants and a halter top, heard her give a little "hmph" under her breath.

Charlie's always talking like that, but he doesn't mean a thing by it. Everybody knows he's faithful as a lapdog to Emmaline, whose daddy after all left him that feed-and-seed store where he's made them a pretty good living the past twenty or so years. It's not like he doesn't have a lot to be grateful for, though I once sat next to Emmaline at a Jaycees' supper and was amazed at how stiff she was able to keep her back and how her top lip was so thin you sometimes couldn't tell if she had one or not. Hope she didn't catch me staring, but I couldn't tear my eyes away— for some reason I found it fascinating, that lip. It does kind of go with the rest of her face, come to think of it, what with that jaw cocked forward, like a bulldog with a certain mind-set.

Funny about Charlie Simpson. He doesn't look romantic or anything. He's some older than me, around forty-five, I guess, and he's not but about five-eight or so. His body's wiry, like the black hairs on his arms, which seem long enough to comb, almost. On top of his head he's missing a fair amount of hair, though that seems to be the only place, and he wears these little gold-rimmed glasses that make him look like an accountant and mostly shade his eyes.

When you get to know him better, you see that Charlie's eyes behind those glasses have silky, dark lashes and heavy lids like that Russian ballet dancer's, lids that look like they're half asleep, or hiding something. Ever since I noticed it, I been torn between wanting to ask him to open his eyes up wide and being afraid of what I might see if he did.

He does have one bad habit, that I know of, which I try my best to overlook. He's always moving his privates around, in front of whoever happens to be standing there. It's not like he does it on purpose or even knows he's doing it. He'll just reach down and take a little dig or rearrange himself, holding a regular conversation all along. Maybe he used to play baseball. I don't know. Tell you one thing, though: it's hard to keep your eyes where they belong and your mind on the discussion at hand, no pun intended.

Charlie says I'm one of the best natural gardeners he ever saw. He can't believe I've only been planting things in a big way like this for a year or so. Must of been hiding my light under a bushel, he says, and when he grins I swear his whole face changes, like electric lights blazing on sudden in the dead of night.

Jimmy Lee says I look like a tomboy in these overalls, and whenever he comes home for lunch and I'm still puttering out there because I sometimes lose track of time in my garden, he pouts like a spoiled little boy. He is, really, which I never said to anybody, though my friend Tootsie Middleton's the first one said it to me. I wouldn't tell Mizz T, though being his momma she's the one ought to know, and me and her have grown closer lately. Just not that close. She did say my flowers're pretty enough for yard of the month, and why didn't I join the garden club. Still, I wouldn't tell her because it wouldn't do any good.

Sitting here at the breakfast table I can see my impatiens blooming their fool heads off underneath the big oak out back. Charlie says the name doesn't mean anything, it's just Latin. But what I think is it means they're impatient as all getout to come up and show their glory, bloom like jewels, even in the shade. I work out there with them every day, even when they don't need watering or weeding. Every day I go out and stroke their gauzy petals, light as wind I stroke them. I think it's magic, the touching.

I love flower names past telling. Been going to the library lately, looking up ideas about gardening. Ginny Knowles, the new librarian, helps me a lot. I sometimes get lost just looking at the names, say them to myself, roll them off my tongue and around in my head till I feel lifted up out of myself.

My friend Tootsie Middleton says that's how she feels in the middle of having sex, when it's right. Lifted up out of herself. Strikes me funny, how loving flowers and making love can stir the same feeling. But I know for a fact that it's true.

Last year, Tootsie up and left behind this town she lived in all her life. Got her the sweetest little apartment in downtown Charleston, had a baby boy she named Louie Blue, I don't know exactly why, and started calling herself Lizbeth, which is short for her real middle name. I paid her a visit a few months back, just to spend one night. Jimmy Lee didn't much like it, sulked for two weeks after, but it was worth it. I wouldn't have traded going for anything, though I did have trouble remembering to call her Lizbeth. And there was that one incident.

Tried to act calm about that trip to Charleston, but to tell you the truth, I don't know when I'd been so excited. Soon as I got on the road, I turned the radio up loud to that rock station Jimmy Lee hates and sang at the top of my lungs. Didn't know the words, but you can guess them and be right half the time. I was hoarse by the time I got to the Cooper River bridge, which I don't mind telling you I'd been fretting over. But once I got up there I wasn't afraid at all, felt like I had wings. Got lost two or three times looking for Tootsie's place, and she had to park my car once I got there, being as the last time I parallel parked was for my driver's test, and then I knocked the stanchion down twice.

"We going out tonight, Till," this after getting me settled, checking out my new turquoise pant suit, and nodding her head like she was satisfied about something. "Going to do the town up." Took the baby to a neighbor's house, and we were off. Had dinner at this little Italian restaurant across from the market where I ate the best garlic bread and drank the best wine I ever tasted. Being there made me think of the last time me and Jimmy Lee were in Charleston. Seemed long ago enough to be another lifetime.

After dinner, Tootsie took me to the Francis Marion Hotel uptown, which is the grandest place, chandeliers big as my living room. We sat at the piano bar. I had a drink called a fuzzy navel, smooth and cool in my throat, and we sang old songs that could almost make you cry they were so sad. The piano player, Harry, said my voice was sweet as spring. And don't I wish the night had stopped there.

When we were getting in our car to go home, somebody hollered across the parking lot to us, came over and put his arm around Tootsie, called her Lizzie-girl, laughed when he saw me and said we surely weren't going home yet, were we, the night was young. Maybe the night was, but I was past it myself, been eating and drinking and singing enough for one night, and, besides, he was no spring chicken, kind of paunchy and jowly and fifty-ish, peering owl eyes looking us over. If we'd come with him, he said, he'd take us somewhere secret. Tootsie leaned over close to me, where I could smell the garlic and bourbon on her breath, saying, "Let's do it, sweetie. Might be fun."

So we followed him in her car. We pulled in and parked behind a huge old building with white columns in front. My eyes were blurry and tired and the only word I could see on the sign when we drove past was "Hibernian," which I never heard of before, but it made me think of bears, so I figured it was probably one of those societies men have, like Jimmy

Lee goes to the Elks and Lions. Turned out I was right, except it's Irish, you could tell by the green stuff everywhere you looked, whenever we went in through the back door.

Only two other people were in there, a man by himself at the bar, plus the bartender. They both looked up and stared when we walked in. The room had a low ceiling and was dark wood paneled everywhere—floor, ceiling, walls. Gave me claustrophobia right off. Between the panels on every wall hung oil paintings, portraits, that is, of men, with brass plaques under each one. The bartender stopped drying glasses and came over to Charlie, that was his name, Charles W. Riley III, and whispered to him kind of urgent. He seemed pretty upset, but Charlie just patted him and took us on into the next room. When we got there he leaned towards Tootsie, his face only about an inch from hers, I could see the space between, and he told her women weren't allowed in this back part, it was tradition, we were in a secret man's place. I got chills all over. Wasn't that worth something, he said, and I saw his hand move, though I couldn't tell what it was up to. Tootsie laughed low and moved back some and I walked away from where they were and looked at the portraits, because here they were again, one face after another looking stern and sour down at me, trespassing on their private, secret place.

Tootsie came over while I was taking the measure of one Archibald McClary, past president of the Hibernian Society, who looked as self-satisfied and

Seeds

safe up there as though he had a notion to live forever, whereas the dates on his plaque made it clear he hadn't.

Tootsie looked kind of wild through the eyes, and her hair was pushed in on one side where she'd leaned against something. "C'mon, Till. Charlie here's got something else to show us." The two of them were giggling how kids do in church. Silly. Still, it was an adventure, and I was ready for that. This was my night for it.

In the dark we walked through high-ceilinged, moonlit rooms. Even though we tiptoed, our steps echoed everywhere. We passed two huge doors, gleaming white, and I realized that must be the front way in. Up a winding staircase we climbed, and I could picture those Charleston debutantes gliding down it, young enough to break your heart, dressed in all their splendor, some fine beau on their arm, fixing to start their lives. High society or no, seem like it all boiled down to the same thing.

By the time we got to the third floor, my fuzzy navel was wearing off and I was ready to sit down, rest a while, and go home. Charlie put a chunky finger to his lips—he had the kind that look like the person doesn't quite have control of them, you know? Kind of loose and blubbery? I hate that kind myself. But he put his finger up there and shhshed me in a wet way, like he knew what I was fixing to say. Then he opened two more tall, wide doors. All I could see was blackness inside.

150

"It's the ballroom, ladies." Charlie's whisper floated by my ear, and in spite of my tiredness I was fascinated, being I'd never seen a ballroom before, much less been in one.

"I'll show you a trick," he said, taking the upper part of my arm and grazing the side of my bosom in the process. I moved away and he held tighter, saying, "Stay by the door, Lizzie. Let me show your little friend something."

It was some lighter there in the hall, and I could see Tootsie's eyes glittering. "Your call, Till."

I leaned towards her and felt a shiver and rush of something pass through me as I whispered back, "Reckon I'll give it a whirl."

Into the darkness we went, Charlie closing the door behind us and pushing me a little ahead of him. Tight as he was, he seemed to know where he was going. We walked in a ways, hundreds of steps it seemed like, and then I felt the pressure of his fingers on my arm loosen and his wet lips graze my cheek. "This ballroom's special, honey." His breath tickled the hairs in my ear and made the little ones on the back of my neck stand up, and I knew that it was true, what he said. "It'll pick up the slightest whisper of sound, from anywhere in here, like magic." He gave me a final squeeze on the arm, saying, "Stay put, honey, I'll show you." Then he was gone, only the faint shuffling of shoes to prove he'd been there at all.

Standing in the dark of that ballroom and feeling all that space around me, seem like suddenly I heard music, a waltz maybe, and smelled the perfume of young girls, their hair swept up and their eyes sparkling like jewels as they twirled, breathless and giddy, from one dance to another, filling their cards with the names of handsome young men, touching lightly the shoulders of young men, searching the smooth, secret faces of their partners, wondering, each time, is he the one? Is this it? My head was spinning, seem like the whole room was filled with the spun sweetness of hopes and dreams, like angel hair, or cotton candy.

I clean forgot about Charlie Riley till the word he whispered came hurtling through the blackness of the Hibernian Hall ballroom. It was the word men use for women's private parts, a short, mean word, full of hard sounds, and it cut through the air like gleaming death, turning that gauzy stuff my mind had spun to cold smoke and scattered ash, leaving behind a stale, familiar smell.

In that unrelieved darkness I stood waiting. Then here came Charlie, though how he found me in the pitch blackness I don't know. I could hear his soft step before I smelled his breath, then he touched my arm, pressed himself full-length against me, and thrust his long, wet tongue into my open mouth.

At the same instant, and without my making a sound, Tootsie opened the door at the front of the ballroom and stuck her head inside. It gave enough light for me to see the big black mole on the side of Charlie Riley's face, beside his right eye, and as I pushed him back with one hand, that's exactly where I aimed with the other.

I was tired, I'd been drinking and singing and climbing stairs, but I still had a fair amount left, judging from the way my fist felt and the howl Charlie Riley let out, which echoed crazily off the ballroom walls. I swung again, just swooshing air that time, then Tootsie was beside me, clucking and hushing us both and asking did we want to get arrested. He never said another word, just covered his one eye and watched me through the other, hung way back coming down the stairs.

Tootsie and I left by the front door this time, left Charles W. Riley III standing at the foot of those winding stairs looking like a poor drunk fool who didn't know what hit him. On the way home she laughed till she wet her pants. After while I laughed, too, though I couldn't shake the bad feeling the whole thing gave me.

Course, I never told Jimmy Lee about it, just said we went out to dinner and spent the rest of the time playing with the baby, which is true. That's all I did the next day, soon as my head eased, that is—played with that sweet, blue-eyed baby. My hand swelled up something awful. Tootsie said that's just how a hand that gets smashed in a car door looks, and it must be, because when I told Jimmy Lee that's what happened, he didn't change words with me. Probably figured it served me right, going off like that.

Didn't feel all that bad lying to Jimmy Lee, even though I hadn't had much practice at it. Used to, I'd tell him everything, more than he wanted to know, I reckon. Always claimed I could talk a thing slam to death. Over the years, I quit doing it. Out loud, anyway. Not much point to it, seem like. Running my mouth into empty space, like pouring seeds on fallow ground.

Why I'm dwelling on all this, I don't know. Guess it's tied up with yesterday. And if I don't get out to my garden soon, it's going to be too hot for watering, and then Jimmy Lee'll be home for lunch, and then I got to grocery shop, and next thing you know the day'll be gone without me getting out there at all. Which is a day lost to me now.

I do love how my gloves and my overalls smell like the garden—not like the flowers. Like dirt. Jimmy Lee makes me hang them out here in the utility room, doesn't want them in the closet with his clothes, he says.

Now here's a funny coincidence: in the nineteen years me and Jimmy Lee been married, I have only twice kissed other men, and they were both named Charlie. Course, that Charlie Riley incident wasn't so much a kiss as it was something else, so maybe that doesn't count. But still.

This time of year, on a morning like this, when you take a deep breath you can smell fall. You know it's still summer, but the air lets you dream of what's coming. I like that. Course, by midday it's so hot you can't remember morning.

That's one of the reasons I love gardening. Teaches me about other things. Isn't any point in getting mad about the heat, for instance. It's coming, and you can't stop it. And it'll go, too, and evenings will come cool again, and mornings fresh. And things you grow will come up and die and come back, if you're lucky. Or not. All you can do is tend what's yours, best you can.

There's this process I read about, that gardeners sometimes use to get flowers ready for transplanting. You hold back from watering, and the soil around the plant gets crusty and cracked, so you might even think it's dead. But it's only getting tough enough to move. The books call that hardening—a notion I find appealing.

Ever since I started going in Charlie Simpson's store, me and him hit it off, till he's got to be what I'd call a friend. Which is something I didn't used to have many of—not that I have a lot now. There's Tootsie, in Charleston, Mizz T, which is unbelievable to me, but true, and there's Charlie—at least I hope there still is, after yesterday. And Ginny Knowles likes me. When I go to the library she shows me books on flowers and gardening. My favorites are the old-fashioned ones, with their pale, delicate drawings and descriptions that glide on the page like poetry.

Whenever Charlie stands near me, pointing out new seed packets or advising the best fertilizer for a certain plant, I can smell him. It's not cologne or aftershave either. It's him. Reminds me of how dirt smells. When I take a deep breath, it's like part of him gets inside me.

Yesterday afternoon in my garden, I was thinking about Charlie, the smell of him and the sweet things he says and his grin and his wiry black hairs and whatever he might be hiding under those heavy lids of his. All the while I was brushing the dirt off my velvet pansy petals, smelling the tang of my geraniums, pinching my petunias and coaxing my moss roses, I was filled up with thoughts of Charlie Simpson. The names of flowers were tumbling through my mind, Latin together with the common, and right in amongst them was Charlie's name, like there wasn't any difference. My head got spinning, so I quit a minute and sat myself under my big oak with the impatiens spreading themselves before me, quilted color. I closed my eyes till I heard a sound, and when I opened them, there stood Charlie. Like I'd conjured him. Which I thought I might've—I have a good imagination and it wouldn't of been the first time I thought I saw something I didn't. So I opened my mouth to say his name, but nothing came out, just a sigh. Then he moved and I saw he was real. It was Charlie.

"Matilda." There's not but two people call me that, and Charlie's one of them. "I . . . brought you that sprinkler you ordered." He had a package in his right hand and with his left he reached down and moved himself from one side to the other. He seemed distracted, and I was plumb taken aback, didn't even know he knew where I lived, though of course that was silly, seeing as how most everybody in Red Hill knows where everybody else lives. I myself have ridden by Charlie Simpson's house I don't know how many times in the past few months.

"Why, Charlie," my voice finally got to working. It came out a little higher pitched than usual, but not so's you'd necessarily remark it. "I clean forgot about that thing." It's not like a new sprinkler head was something I really needed, but I did remember ordering it. Jimmy Lee says I got to stop spending his hard-earned money at the farm store—that's what he calls Charlie's place, with a nasty little edge behind his voice, which used to worry me, but which I've taken to ignoring anymore.

"No need to get up, Matilda," Charlie started backing away as I braced my feet against the ground and my back against the tree. "I was just, I can just, I got to . . ." He couldn't get the words out and he all of a sudden realized it, so he gave up, just hushed and shrugged and then grinned, broad enough to light the shade under my oak.

I smiled back and he relaxed some and said how healthy my impatiens looked and I said to come see that hybrid geranium I been working on and we walked around in my garden for about fifteen minutes, him calling the names of my flowers and remarking on my mulch and holding that sprinkler in his hand and every once in a while rearranging himself. Wouldn't look at me, though, just at my plantings. I asked wouldn't he like some lemonade and he said he had to go and I said why not stay for a little cooling off, because by this time it was hot, the time of day I usually rest inside, and he finally said he would, but he had to get on back to the store soon, it'd have to be a quick one.

I didn't have a thing in my mind except lemonade when I went in the kitchen, though I did sneak a quick look at myself in the bathroom mirror. Thought about brushing my hair but there wasn't much use in it, being it was plastered to my head on account of sweat.

Fixed drinks and went to the backyard. Charlie was propped up against the oak, right where I'd been sitting, looking comfortable for the first time since he'd got here. There's only a small spot of bare ground under that tree, and when I sat down cross-legged, I took up the rest of the space, and seem like the shade and the oak and the flowers folded us in there, secret and safe.

Looking at the sweat beaded on Charlie's top lip made me think of things, so I turned my eyes away and looked at his hand on the lemonade glass, at the way those black, wiry hairs curled on his squared-up thumb, which had dirt under the nail. Then I looked up at Charlie's eyes, which is about the time I realized neither one of us had said a word since I brought the lemonade. Inside me something shifted—I put my lemonade glass down, pushed forward with my knees, put one arm on either side of Charlie where he sat against the tree and pressed my lips to his. Seem like it was slow motion and I was the only one moving. Up till the time I would of had to go cross-eyed, I kept my eyes open, so I could see that Charlie did, too, watching me through his glasses and those half-lidded eyes of his, not surprised, but not expecting it either. Just as I closed my eyes, I felt myself starting to rise up. In the second we touched, my mind thought of his smell and the feel of his lips and the roughness of the tree bark under my palms. And then he opened his mouth and I opened mine and thinking stopped. We kissed a kiss that lasted till I felt like I'd drowned and died in it. Charlie never moved his hands to hold me and I never moved mine off the tree—we were just connected at the mouth, and it went on forever. Must've breathed sometime, but I don't remember doing it. I could smell flowers and dirt and Charlie and myself, and colors and names and smells and feelings circled in my head, like nothing I ever felt before.

However long it took, when it was over, seem like we both knew it at the same time. I rocked back on my heels and picked up my glass. Charlie sipped at his lemonade long enough to be polite and then said he best be getting back to the store.

What's funny is, I don't love Charlie Simpson, though I think he's a sweet man and I'm past grateful to him for yesterday. Maybe I should feel guilty about kissing him, but I don't. Instead I feel like I discovered a delicious secret about myself, one that's been buried so far down I didn't know it was there. And I'm not sure of its proper name, that rising-up thing inside me, but I'm calling it passion. And it's mine, I have it. All I got to figure now is what to do with it.

Mizz T and Me

Yesterday Mizz T died. I was with her. She gave me a gift just before. I returned the favor best I could, but I don't know if it makes us even.

Spent the first seventeen years of my marriage hating the woman. Spent the last three getting to know her. And it is nothing short of amazing to look across that stretch of time and see her and myself as the same people we became.

Died of asbestosis, which is this man-made kind of cancer, lies quiet inside a long time and then runs through you like a hellbent train. Bubbles up black in your lungs till you can't swallow or breathe, then strangles you. Closest anybody can figure, Mizz T got exposed whenever she worked a little while as a clerk in the Charleston shipyards, during the war. They don't know, just guessing. Doesn't alter her being dead, anyhow.

It's quick, that's one thing. Three months ago today they told her she'd have about three months. Pretty good—getting to where they can guess when you're going out good as they can guess when you're coming in. In-between is what's tricky.

For Mizz T and me, the part in between hating and loving was lengthy and unpleasant. And I reckon if I could have things over I'd try to do different, but, on the other hand, you can't get where you are without going through what you did.

After that one Christmas when I first called her Mizz T to her face and she first smiled a real smile at me, the two of us started being cordial. Over time, we practiced being friendly to each other. And when Celeste divorced Ham, permed her hair up frizzy, and moved to California, it seemed to mark a milestone for us. We were the only two women left in the Turner clan—discounting Celeste and Ham's daughter Margaret, who was busy getting married—and it seemed natural that we would grow closer. Natural or not, that's what happened.

It was gradual, of course. I called Mizz T for a recipe; she asked me over for coffee. I mended a blouse because her stiff, bent fingers couldn't hold a needle proper; she baked me a cake on my birthday. First time anybody'd done that since I was a little girl.

Soon we visited together three or four times a week. Jimmy Lee didn't know what to make of it, but he was mostly pleased. Eased the pressure on him some. Hadn't been for me, he'd of been the one it fell to, taking the edge off his momma's loneliness.

Sure wasn't a one-sided deal, though. Mizz T was helping me make up a cycle I'd missed. Some emptiness that'd been in me a long time started filling up.

Last year, right before Mizz T got sick, Margaret had her first child. Soon as they got home from the hospital, I took Mizz T for a visit. All the way over in the car, she couldn't keep still—thin, pale hands fluttering from her face to her lap and back again, clasping each other—she was most beside herself. "A girl, Mattie. A little Turner girl. Can you believe it?"

She didn't need me to remind her Margaret's little girl was not a Turner but a Szarnowski instead, that being the name of the Yankee Margaret'd met in college and married despite all the threats her daddy could muster. Or to say that Margaret was a Turner girl, too. What mattered to Mizz T wasn't the last name anyhow. It was the middle one, Estelle—Mizz T's own name.

Margaret and Stan rent a little house over in Baytown, and driving through there made me feel a longing for the old days, before I knew how things would turn out. When we walked in, Margaret was on the sofa, still in her gown, with the baby's white wicker bassinet right there beside her. She looked happy to me, even with those dark circles under her eyes. Mizz T didn't even glance in her direction, made a beeline for that bassinet instead, jostling it so that the baby woke up right off and cried.

Mizz T wanted to hold the baby just that minute, but Margaret said she was hungry and wet, so we waited while she changed her, then opened her gown and offered her breast, graceful and unself-conscious as if she's in the room by herself. I'd never seen a nursing baby before, and it took me by surprise, how it's so beautiful it makes you ache.

Finally she finished, Mizz T fidgeting to beat the band the whole time. I could see Margaret was some nervous, but her grandmomma was hellbent to hold that baby, and it wouldn't be fair not to let her. I settled Mizz T in the big green armchair, which had support on both sides, then Margaret lifted that tiny baby and placed her ever so careful in Mizz T's waiting arms. Margaret and I both held our breaths, but we needn't have worried. Because Mizz T's nervousness and shaking quit altogether, minute she got that great-grandbaby in her arms. She grew still and quiet, murmuring something we couldn't make out. There was such a sweetness in her face. I wanted to hold that baby myself, but I didn't move or breathe, just sat still, trying to keep that picture in my head.

I wondered, how did that trip happen? The one from holding a baby like that, with a feeling like the one on Mizz T's face, to being seventy-five years old and having her babies, grown men now, think she was just too much trouble. Shouldn't they be holding her sweetly, the way she must've held them? Hadn't she earned the right?

Mizz T went downhill fast, once the cancer'd been named. Wanted to stay home, she said, die where she'd lived fifty-some years. I went over every day, and we got a nurse to help out, but it finally got too hard and we had to move her. By then she didn't know where she was half the time anyway. But still she hated being alone, so after a couple days I rented a cot and slept next to her hospital bed.

Last three weeks she got so frail, weighed eighty-some pounds. Skin stretched smooth, bones came up, till her face'd put you in mind of a baby bird's. Hair wispy as a newborn's, skin so thin I could see her whole tracery of veins. Which was beautiful to me, in a strange way. I'd stroke her lightly with my fingertips, and she'd smile sometimes, make a small, sweet noise that I liked hearing.

Those were the quiet times, right after medication. Seem like Mizz T was my baby then. I held her to my breast, crooned a quiet lullaby, and rocked her. And thought to myself, thank you, Lord.

In the bad times Mizz T'd choke on that slick, black liquid in her lungs. She'd try to get up, to breathe, to cough it out. She'd fight, kick the bed-clothes off. But she wasn't strong enough. I'd sit her up, hold her shoulders, and straighten her. Then it'd come boiling up, that dark poison. Stop a few minutes and start again.

She'd cough, and if Jimmy Lee was visiting, he'd leave the room while I held a gold plastic basin under her chin and wiped her face with a cool washcloth. Ham hardly ever came at all, said somebody had to keep the store going. But I could see from the look on his face when he did come that he couldn't take it. And I was sorry for him.

Mizz T was clear sometimes, between the wearing off of the medicine and the attacks. She'd pat my hand and tell me stories about Ham and Jimmy Lee in a whispery voice. Like that time they surprised her with a birthday cake they baked themselves, when they were teenagers. I knew about that, Jimmy Lee mentioned it once. Missed her birthday by a month. She didn't tell that part.

She'd be in and out, saying something reasonable one minute, crazy the next. Once she stroked my face, called me her baby. Made my breath come short.

One of the last things Mizz T whispered to me before she quit trying altogether was that she's leaving her house to me and Jimmy Lee. Which was surprising enough in itself, I reckon. Always figured Ham'd get it, being the oldest. But the real surprise was this: I have me thirty thousand dollars. Mizz T's left me that, the principal on her inheritance from her momma, which she never touched. When she said I'd gotten to be like a daughter to her, I had a feeling she was thinking about that girl baby who got twisted up inside her and strangled on her cord. I been strangling, too, it hit me then, and I almost said it, almost asked her, did she know.

But I don't think so, else maybe she just couldn't admit it.

Lord, how she did love Jimmy Lee. Her last-born, and she knew it. Didn't ever make him do anything on his own. She couldn't see how that hurt him. And his daddy couldn't see past Ham, a copy of himself.

Those Turner men never have understood the first thing about women. Jimmy Lee's always just followed the example of his daddy and his brother. Women are a convenience for them, like a power tool maybe, only not quite as handy. Give you an example, down at the store, about four years ago, Ham and Jimmy Lee started paging their employees, who are all women, using numbers—like "Number 3, tele-phone," or "Number 6, call the office"—instead of names. Got the idea from K-Mart. Their daddy would of loved it. It's how I feel at home sometimes, like a number. I said that to Jimmy Lee once, and he asked me was I going to start being one of those libbers.

I remember that time he called me a bitch, under his breath, but loud enough for me to hear. When he did, I wondered to myself if it was so, was I one. Decided I probably was, because hearing it made me feel so.

Used to think one or two circumstances shape our lives, make us what we finally become. Figured losing my baby and them taking my womb out were my two. Now I see it *is* those things, plus all the little ones we can't add up. And it's also that we never finally *become* at all. We change. It's one of the things I learned from Tootsie Middleton. Then Mizz T showed me: she was changing up to the minute she died.

She gave me more than half her house and that money, you know. Gave me seventeen years of grief and misery first. Then at the end she gave me her real gift—the chance to be her daughter, to be her momma, to help her die, to complete some full circle that has changed me forever. Gave me her name: I'm Mizz T, too, if I care to be. She let me see her life clearly. It's how I've come to know I want something else.

Wish I knew if she meant to do it.

What I gave Mizz T in return was a lie to die with. It was the most I could do. Wasn't a made-up lie. I just let her keep the one she'd been living with for years.

She was real close, I could tell. She was tired, and, Lord, so was I.

"Jimmy Lee still here?" She whispered that to me. I could barely hear it. He'd only been there twice in three days, for about ten minutes all told.

Mizz T couldn't get her eyes open to see now and she hadn't been able to hear much for years, but she could still *feel*. Bent my face down close to hers so she could feel the warmth of my breath. Picked up one of her fine, blue hands, light as a dream, put two of her fingers up against my lips so she could feel me telling her. I said: "Yes ma'am, Mizz T, he's right here."

Soon as I fed those words from my lips to her fingers, she let out a sigh, the pain drained away, and she nestled her head down into the pillow. Looked sweet and dreamy: like a baby, sleeping. I touched the skin of her cheek with my finger. It was soft and still warm. I will never forget that particular texture of skin.

Spent the morning pondering that lie, her life, and my own. Now I got to rouse myself and get to work. Because I'm not quite through with Mizz T yet. There's arrangements to be made, and I'm the one's making them.

Reunion

"Momma!" I holler. I'd of known her anywhere. Even from a distance of twenty-one years, even after two hours in the air for my very first time plus two on the ground in Atlanta that were like a trip into the next century. Even with my ears stopped up from the ride and my heart beating most out of my chest.

When last I saw her, my momma was a tall and graceful woman. I still remember the way Daddy'd sometimes take her in his arms and bend her backwards in our kitchen, her waist curving like the stalk of a flower—so many years ago now it seems like another lifetime. Remember the sound of her laugh, and his, like music blending, and feeling like I should leave, and staying, watching, hungering for something.

Whenever I thought of Momma, through the years, that's how I saw her. Whenever I tried to make myself think of her getting older, I pictured her growing taller maybe, and thinner — thinning right out, going paler and paler till you might not see her at all. Will-o'-the-wisp.

But I'd had it all wrong. Because here she is before me, and she's the same — same long, thin neck; same slim, graceful body. And now, after all these years, she's wearing her dark hair down again. Like a young girl, she looks. Like time stopped for her.

Feel a burning in my throat, and I'm afraid, like something terrible's fixing to erupt. But it's too late to turn back, so I call out again, walking towards her all the time through the crowd of people waiting to greet their loved ones. She won't look at me, though, even when I call, just keeps craning her neck to someplace behind me.

"Momma!" I near scream it finally, a sound so harsh my throat aches, my own voice surprising me and filling me with something like panic — people turning their heads and clearing a path like the parting of the Red Sea — and still she won't stop that craning. And me all the time moving towards her in slow motion like those TV commercials where the man and woman are running towards each other in a field. Almost there; feel my face working and can't make it quit.

Then on my arm comes a touch. Light, I almost don't feel it at all. Turn my head slightly to the side and there stands a woman staring at me with a questioning look, a thick-waisted, dark-haired woman, no taller than me, eyes wide and cheeks puffed out like she's been snakebit, full at the jaws with some hard-luck lines running down between her nose and mouth. I glance over once more towards the slim young woman, who's hugging some young man, and then of course I know. A roaring's in my ears, maybe from the plane ride. Just before I drop my bag and purse to hug this dark-haired stranger, I look into her eyes and see she's scared half witless, same as me.

That's how my visit with Momma kicked off last week, a visit that came about on account of this overwhelming urge to see her, started the day we buried Mizz T and wouldn't let up till I did something about it. Called and asked could I come, she asked Mr. Jackson and then said yes. Told Jimmy Lee I was going, which made him moan one more time about how he didn't know what got into his momma, leaving me all that money. Which is about the umpteenth time he's said it. Boy needs to move on. Still, he did take me to the airport.

Which brings me to how come I'm sitting here five days later, looking out one of these funny little rounded windows, studying cloud patterns and trying not to catch the eye of the sweet little lady on my right, looks like she wants more than anything to tell me her life's story, which I don't have time for just now. Too busy contemplating my own.

Lord, Momma looked different. Not that I expected she'd look the same. Twenty-one years is a long time. But it wasn't just her looks—her whole *self* seemed changed. She didn't even smell like I remembered, and I always thought a person's smell was permanent and unchangeable, like fingerprints. But I see now my mistake, for there is nothing in this world unchangeable.

Like our meeting in the airport, for example, with her looking at me for once and me looking somewhere else—the exact opposite of how we'd done all our lives up to then.

"Earl said it'd be a miracle if you got here on time, but you did, didn't you?" She was breathless as a young girl as we pulled out of the airport parking lot.

"Earl said you'd be tired, and I reckon you are, it's not easy, flying today, what with planes being bombed right and left and crashing and . . ." She let that thought drift off into nothing.

I wasn't being quiet on purpose. It's just that now I was finally here I couldn't seem to get my mouth working. Which problem she did not have. Silence seemed to get on her nerves, so she kept steady talking all the way to their place.

"Earl says if they keep letting all these kids in here, we're going to have to find us another area," she offered as we pulled into their development and parked in front of their condo, a tan-and-brown two-story. Far as the eye could see were other condos just like it.

"But you know how the condo market is," she continued, smiling crooked over at me, eyes flitting every whichway. Truth is, I don't know one thing about the condo market, nor even how a person finds her house after dark in a place like this—

weren't any numbers I could see. I imagined myself wandering from one tan-and-brown condo to the next, knocking on the wrong doors, looking for home. Person could do it for months in a place like this, seem like.

"Yes ma'am," I said.

"Earl said he figured us girls'd need time to ourselves—catching up time, he calls it." She was fitting her key into the lock and smiling shyly over her shoulder at me. "He had Masons tonight anyhow. Won't be home till late."

Course, Mr. Jackson didn't have to be there in person, what with Momma's constant rendering of his thoughts on everything from real estate development to air fresheners.

"Earl says there must be some aerosol would take care of this smell," she said as we stepped into a tiny, dark hall. Which smell I didn't need to ask—it filled my lungs the minute we walked in, strong and sharp enough to bring tears. "But I have yet to find one can do the job."

With airplane glue, according to Momma, the best you can do is ventilate, ventilate, ventilate. "That's how come we have ceiling fans in every room," she explained proudly, as we proceeded through the dining room, into the living room, and up the stairs, her flipping on lights and fans as we went. Tiny pieces of airplane covered every flat surface in the place: the dining room table, the bookshelf in the hall, every table in the living room, even the top of the TV.

As we went upstairs, the odor got stronger. "Smell rises, just like heat," Momma said, though I hadn't asked.

"Earl moved most of his stuff out of here for your visit." She showed me into a small bedroom which had been green-and-yellow-ginghamed near to death. "Don't open the closet, though, hear?"

I stood in the middle of the room, holding my bags and blinking in the light, which flickered something fierce on account of the ceiling fan. The smell of glue had me dizzy.

"Soon's you freshen up we can have supper," she said.

We ate baked beans and franks sitting at the kitchen bar on account of the table being too cluttered. While we ate, Momma told how, after his retirement the year before, Mr. Jackson had taken up model airplane building. "Earl says retired people who don't have hobbies just curl up and die," she said.

What Momma had taken up for herself, as it turns out, was religion. Which wasn't that much of a surprise because besides the glue, the other thing you couldn't miss in their place was the collection of crosses and renderings of the crucifixion. They were in every room, including the hall bathroom, where He hung opposite the medicine cabinet, so you couldn't even brush your teeth in peace. The picture over the guest-room bed showed a Jesus with the look of a maniac, hanging up there on that cross, face

twisted, eyes rolled back in his head. Made you feel
like he needed to be up there, for the good of society.

Momma said she'd gone to church with a neighbor the year before, just about the time Mr. Jackson
retired, and got saved. When she said it, her whole
face smoothed out. It was enough to make you
believe it, if you didn't think too hard about the
pictures.

It wasn't easy, Momma told me, raising those three
girls, but they finally got grown and left, and somehow seemed to of turned out all right. "I'm a grandmother four times over," she said proudly, like it was
an accomplishment she had something to do with.

Whole time she was talking, I studied her face,
trying to see the woman I kept in my mind all those
years. The one my daddy'd loved so, whose laugh my
memory heard clear as rain, whose soft hair I could
still conjure the smell of. Who cried in my arms, and
left me. That slim betrayer I harbored grief for. Hard
as I looked, I couldn't see.

Later, as I lay in her guest-room bed, my head filled
with glue-smell and the whir of the fan, I decided that
other was somebody I either invented — like the slim
young woman I'd called to that day at the airport —
else one who'd died somewhere along the way, with
me not there to witness. This woman I was visiting
was nice enough, I thought — somebody who'd
worked hard to find a place for herself, made the best
she could of what was given her. Who was I to
criticize that? Tossing and turning in that green and
yellow bed in the shadow of that crazed and suffering

portrait, I came to the conclusion that Momma hadn't had much luck at her new life. And maybe I fell asleep feeling just.

Over the next two days Mr. Jackson stayed pretty clear of us. We went sightseeing to the mall, visited Momma's church group, and exchanged a few facts about each other's lives that hadn't come up in twenty-one years of phone calls and letters. But mostly we were polite and distant as strangers in a waiting room.

Day before I was scheduled to come home, we had visitors—Mr. Jackson's oldest, Tonya, with her two kids. Tonya'd been about eight last time I saw her, and here she was almost thirty, a fact which near took my breath away. She was cute enough, looked something like her daddy, dark hair and a nose about an inch longer than it needed to be. Kind of sullen around the mouth. Working on her second marriage. Momma'd filled me in on all that.

Tonya's girl Suzie was ten now, Little Earl barely two and still in diapers—dirty ones, judging by the odor, which was strong enough to work its way through the smell of glue and baking apples. Momma was in the kitchen making a pie for that night. Mr. Jackson was going to join us at a meal for the first time since I got there. My goodbye dinner. Me and Tonya sat on barstools across the counter from Momma, drinking Coke and trying to talk over the noise of Little Earl, who hung on his momma's neck the entire time, hollering in her ear, while Suzie sat by herself in the living room behind us, watching cartoons, the volume turned high enough to compensate for Little Earl.

When Tonya said she had to go, I almost hugged her neck, I was so grateful. We walked her to the front door, Momma wiping her hands on a dish towel, Little Earl still smelly and loud, Suzie following silent and watchful. When we got there, Tonya turned around, hugged my momma, and said, "OK, Mom. See you next week."

"OK, sweetie." Momma's face wrinkled up in a smile. "Take care, hear?" No more words than that, but I knew in a rush howled through me like wind on a desert how much the two of them had shared. In the midst of which knowing, I caught Suzie's dark eyes resting steady on mine. Then she smiled for the first time and said, "Bye, Aunt Mattie." And just like that, I'd lost a momma and gained a niece, which two events left me plumb winded, like a one-two punch.

That night the three of us ate glazed ham and sweet potatoes in the living room, balancing our plates on our laps and clearing space for our glasses in between tiny wings and propellers.

"Earl says people tend to overcook ham," Momma explained, through bites of some of the sweetest, tenderest meat I about ever tasted. Me and Earl just kept eating, proving she hadn't made that mistake.

"Sweet potatoes are just about the perfect food, Earl says." Truth is, everything Earl said came out of my momma's mouth. I was wondering to myself when he ever got the chance to say any of it.

Over coffee and pie, though, Earl did finally talk. Told how fascinating it is, putting those planes together, getting the paint just right. "Recreating history," he said, and I saw Momma's lips move, repeating his words to herself, storing them up for later.

Earl went on up, me and Momma did dishes, then settled down for a last cup. It was the most relaxed we'd been the whole visit. From Earl's recliner where I sat, the lamplight softened her face and slimmed her jaw, and as she raised the cup to her lips and smiled, I suddenly saw her again, my young momma of memory. And was rocked back in time like twenty-one years wasn't any more than an hour. At just that moment, she leaned forward as though to touch me, saying, "It's been good, Sister, having you visit."

"I'm not your sister, Momma." The words flung themselves out before I could think, scattered in the room bitter and brittle as the glue-soaked airplane parts we sat surrounded by.

Her hand shot back to her lap and in the lamplight her eyes glittered. "I surely do know that, Mattie." She put her cup down and cradled one hand inside the other, twisting them and looking down. "Why, I can remember like it was yesterday, the day I bore you. Can see the look on your daddy's face, so proud."

It was the first time his name'd been mentioned. She looked up from her lap, right into my face, tears falling in streams. "Oh, didn't we think we'd live forever then, and be happy, and together."

Seemed to gather herself, took in a deep breath, and let it out slow. "Turned out in the end, though, didn't it? Hadn't you made a right good life for yourself?" And looking into that face that seemed to hold past and present inside itself, it was suddenly like I saw myself sitting there, years of hope and disappointment, grief and joy, guilt and discovery reflected in a face that was and wasn't what I thought it should be. Thought of Jimmy Lee, and Mizz T's legacy, of babies I wanted and never had, of Tootsie and Ginnie, and my garden. Inside my own self, I felt something loosen and let go.

"Yes ma'am," I said, looking away from her.

After a little bit we went to bed, and I dreamed of my daddy for the first time in years — a dream where he wasn't choking or hungry, just at peace.

When Momma left me at the airport today, saying she'd be in touch and we'd have to do this again soon, I said the same thing. And maybe it's even true.

Evening's fading into night now. In less than thirty minutes, Jimmy Lee'll be picking me up at the airport, asking me how did it go. Wonder will I tell him I'm ready to give truth to the lie I told my momma last night.

We left Atlanta a while back, the plane rising up hard like they do. Soon as it and my stomach level off some, I look out my window. The sun's heading off, taking its glory under the clouds. I look across the aisle, through the other window, and there shines the moon, fixing to parade her pale self. And in between're me and all the rest of the people on this trip, never reflecting the same light twice.

Cleaning House

Water's dripping somewhere, echoing through this half-empty house and into my brain like a reminder of who knows what. When you turn the faucet on, nothing comes out. They say it'll be days or maybe even weeks before we have anything simple as running water. But it's starting to lighten up outside— from my bed I see shadows and shapes, outlines of things that used to be familiar—so it'll be light enough soon for me to go see can I find where that dripping's coming from.

Who can say where things come from anyhow? Like the crazy red anger rose up in me two days ago, one wave of it after another, railing against twenty-two years worth of memory. Or the howling wind named Dion, changed the face of our house and our lives and this town overnight.

This morning, though, where things come from

carries less weight with me than where they're going.

Like me, I'm going somewhere, soon's light comes and I can pack a few things—provided they get the roads cleared, that is. Don't exactly know where, just out of the path of destruction, quick as I can get. Which who knows how far I'll have to go.

Didn't much think I was going far two days ago, standing in my kitchen, packing up our earthly belongings for what Jimmy Lee claimed would be the last time, fixing to move the few blocks over to Mizz T's place, take up that legacy of hers. All morning long, every time I wrapped something in newspaper and put it in a box, I'd think back to when we got it, connecting up twenty-two years of *things*. Like they had their own meaning, like they could make sense of our lives.

I knew there's a storm brewing, it'd been on the radio for days. Tropical depression gone bad, name of Dion, which to me was about as lame a name as you could conjure, but maybe they ran short in the early letters, else somebody was satisfying a leftover teen-age urge. Better to hang it on a hurricane than some poor child, I reckon.

Not that I gave Dion much thought. Just kept packing, figuring we'd have us a few days of rain, which we could use it, being's this fall's been dry as bones.

I was wrapping the creamer to our good china which had been stored away so long I forgot we had it. It was Mizz T's standard present to me for years, pieces of china I just put away in one closet or another as we moved from house to house. Saving it for good. That's how people do, till when they die you find closets and chests full of good things hadn't seen the light of day in years. Don't care for the pattern, didn't pick it out or anything, it just started appearing, one piece after the other. Twenty-two years worth of china I didn't want.

And there I was, wrapping it up to move again. Into Mizz T's house, where it could sit in one of her china cabinets, be found there when I die.

It was a funny feeling, wrapping that china and thinking about living there, a house I'd felt uncomfortable in for so many years, which had seen me married, witnessed holidays and birthdays, funerals and christenings. Thinking about twenty-two years of Jimmy Lee saying c'mon, and me dragging along behind him from one place to the next. And now headed for Mizz T's, the top of the heap, pure white and grand, with its wide green lawn, manicured as a movie star's hands, and that avenue of oaks, as she liked to call it, leading up to the house. Lord, hadn't I spent many a miserable hour in there.

Course, for Jimmy Lee, it's like going home, somewhere he's been looking to go all along. I could see us both, aging inside that house, me turning into Mizz T, choking to slow death, while Jimmy Lee grew senile, returning to a boyhood he hadn't ever strayed that far from anyhow.

I was about half through the cups—delicate handled and so little you couldn't get but about two swallows of coffee out of them—not that anybody swallows whenever they drink out of something like

this, they sip instead—when in busts Jimmy Lee
through the back door.

"Storm's coming, Mat." He's wild-eyed and
excited. "Lester Turnbull says it's the big one." Lester's the civil defense warden for Red Hill, and he
lives for hurricane season; been predicting the big
one long as anybody can remember.

It's hot in our kitchen, and stuffy. I finish the cup
I'm wrapping and wipe sweat from my face.

"You got to get over to Momma's." He looks
around the kitchen like he's wondering what to carry
with him. "It's making landfall tonight."

And when he says it I get a picture of a huge wall of
water, rising up past imagining, making land fall
beneath it till it disappears like it was never there. Feel
a shiver run all through me, like I don't know we're
ninety miles inland.

"We're ninety miles inland, Jimmy Lee." As I pick
up the next cup and start wrapping, my hands're
steady, though black with the print of old news.

"You got to take care of Momma's house," he says
again as he paces the kitchen, pent-up and red-faced.
"Me and Ham're staying down at the store." He's
heading down the hall now, his voice floating back to
me where I stand wrapping. "Case of looters."

I can't help it, I snort out loud at that one. Which
Jimmy Lee doesn't hear, he's upstairs now, I hear
footsteps above me, then water running.

He's at the hall closet, I hear him rummaging.
When he shows his face again, his golf clubs slung
over one shoulder, he knits up his forehead. "Hear,

Mattie? Grab a few things and get on over to Momma's. There's more to save there." He shifts from one foot to the other. "Turn the water off, too, when the bathtub's full. Might need it later."

I place the wrapped cup into the box with the others, a little too hard, I guess, because I hear the slightest grating noise as I fit it into place, and I know the delicate handle has separated itself from the cup.

What is it makes something happen? I can't say. Just a piling of one event on another, I reckon. Pressure building up quiet underneath till it has to come boiling out, like with volcanoes or earthquakes. Or Lizzie Borden's murdering rage. Else just a chance series of events, like two clouds bumping into each other way across the ocean and teaming up to blow a fierce wind three thousand miles. Doesn't have to be big, the thing that starts it. It can be harmless as light reflecting off the head of a nine iron, or the set of a hand on a hip. All of a sudden your whole life shifts, and you do something.

For me it was the grating of that china cup, separating itself in two. I look down from where Jimmy Lee stands in the doorway, a redness filling my head, a buzzing starting up at the base of my skull, sending a vibration right through me.

My hands're still steady, though, as I unwrap the cup. It can be saved, I see that right off: a clean break that can be glued till you could hardly see the cracks, glued and set back on some shelf where, to look at it, you'd never know the difference. It's not like anybody's using it anyhow.

Then the vibration in my head reaches my hands. As I watch, they set up a motion like a motorcycle engine idling, making the handle clink against the cup. Which noise joins the buzzing in my head, making a terrible harmony.

The bone white cup gives up then, leaps from its bed of newspaper to the floor, leaving the handle behind, splintering into a thousand shards you could spend a lifetime trying to put back together, if you'd a mind to.

And maybe that would of been enough, that one cup breaking—I could've swept it up and thrown it out without dwelling on it—if I didn't happen to glance up just that second to see Jimmy Lee heave a big sigh, like he's the world's most put-upon person. Doesn't say a word, just sighs hard enough to shift the golf clubs on his shoulder. And as the light reflects off the face of his nine iron, I suddenly realize that of all the things in our house, Jimmy Lee has chosen to save what means the most to him.

My hands dive down into the box of wrapped china, lighting on a dinner plate. I don't have to take my eyes off Jimmy Lee to know that. I can feel its shape and weight as my hands undo their own work. Holding the empty plate out to Jimmy Lee a moment, I offer it up, like there might be something he could fill it with. And him just blinking, fixing to open his mouth to say something. But we neither of us'll ever know what, since before he can utter a sound, that plate flies from my outstretched hand into the wall to the left of Jimmy Lee's head. Pretty far to the left, too, though you wouldn't know it by how he jumps.

"Jesus Christ, Mat." His hand comes off his hip to rest on the door jamb. "What in hell'd you do that for?"

Above our heads I hear the bathtub filling. Outside the sun is brilliant, giving the lie to rumors of storm on this fine fall afternoon. I hear a bird chirp, and the echo of that grinding, separating sound. I hear Jimmy Lee's breathing, ragged and surprised. Inside myself, I hear my heart, and I am filled suddenly with a rising-up feeling I have come to recognize.

My voice, mild and quiet, says words I don't expect. "I'm unpacking, Jimmy Lee."

Sounds reasonable enough, if you don't think about what my hands are doing. My whole body has set up a shaking now, and before I can aim the next plate, it jumps from my hand, seems to shatter in midair before it even makes landfall. I reach into the box again and this time my hands find a salad plate which manages to end where I aim, the front of the cabinet where our tall, thin wineglasses stand enclosed in glass, like they thought it was protection enough. I am in a rhythm now, my hands expert at unwrapping and hefting, when Jimmy Lee drops his clubs, strides across the room and almost touches me. He looks into my eyes a minute. I don't know what he sees, but I see his widen. Then he drops his hand and goes back to the doorway, silent witness.

This unwrapping is slowing me up, so I lift the whole box off the kitchen table—it's still heavy, only half unpacked—and through the buzzing in my head I think I hear Jimmy Lee holler something at the exact moment that I let it fall to my feet. It gives off a wonderfully satisfying sound, that china. The rest of the dishes are sitting on the table waiting to be wrapped and put away. With one arm, how they do in the movies sometimes, I sweep them to the floor. They crunch under my feet as I make my way over to the cabinet, reach in through the broken glass, pick up glasses and dishes and throw them, one at a time, wherever it suits me: on the floor, against the wall, at the ceiling. The kitchen is covered with dishes waiting to be put in boxes, lined up like bean bags for target practice at a county fair. Sitting ducks, and me a woman with a mission. The more I throw, the better I get. With a Corning Ware casserole dish, I knick enamel from our side-by-side refrigerator/freezer. A milk pitcher, used to belong to Jimmy Lee's grand-momma, dents the microwave door.

I look over at my husband then, at whom, I'll have you know, I've not aimed a single piece of anything. His jaw's gaped open like a fish's. He stands ready to run. Inspired, I grab his favorite coffee mug, the heavy ceramic one, special made, with the store's name and emblem on it. We both watch it fly end-over-end till it hits its mark, that ugly glass vase was a gift years back from Ham and Celeste, sending the both of them to kingdom come. At that, Jimmy Lee can't contain himself. He croaks out, "My God, Mat. I believe you've lost your mind."

I'm gazing at him, a heavy soup tureen in my hand, hefted about ear level, when I see a big splat of water hit his forehead and roll down his face. We both look up at the same time to see a dark spreading circle on the ceiling above him. As we watch, another large drop hits him square between his upturned eyes. Which strikes me so funny I laugh out loud, a short, sharp bark.

"Jesus Christ. The bathtub." He tears down the hall and upstairs. Just as the water stops running, there comes a huge crash and the dark circle is now a gaping hole, pieces of plaster and gallons of water gushing through it to land on our kitchen floor, which makes it easy to hear Jimmy Lee cussing and moaning up there, and by now I'm laughing so hard I can barely stand up, it's too funny.

In a minute, I look up to see Jimmy Lee back at the doorway, standing stock still, surveying the mess like he can't believe his eyes—looking over at me holding my stomach and laughing. Puts one hand on his hip again, saying, "Now look what you've done," which looks so silly and makes me so mad I take aim with the tureen at the light fixture hanging over the kitchen table. And somewhere between my being doubled over laughing and trying to straighten up enough to throw, Jimmy Lee disappears, leaving everything behind. I look out the window in time to see his car turn the corner, fast enough to make the tires squeal.

Just like that my laughing's over, and I'm suddenly

tired enough to lie down right there on my kitchen floor. Too tired to throw the tureen, even.

Looking down at my arms I see they're bleeding, cut on the soft inside part from reaching into the cabinet. I make my way upstairs like a person walking under water, bandage myself, and fall into bed. Just before my eyes close, I see sunlight reflected off the ceiling and the treetops swaying in a soft breeze.

Seem like midnight when I woke, it was so dark. But the clock beside my bed told me it was only eight, usually still light enough to see. Then I heard it, what I'd been hearing since I woke but hadn't registered—the phone ringing above the sound of wind, steady, loud and rising.

"Hello?"

"Mat." He sounded breathless. "They just upgraded it to a four. You got to get over to Momma's while you still can."

Outside one gust of wind stood out from the rest, threatening and blustery. I heard something drop and roll, a garbage can maybe.

"Supposed to hit around midnight, Mat. You got to go."

"Why would I be better off by myself at your momma's house, Jimmy Lee, than by myself at my own?" He didn't answer. Between us the phone line crackled.

"I'm staying put," I said, my voice surprising me by how sure it sounded. "We can talk in the morning." What I wasn't sure about was what we'd have to say. Figured I'd have the night to consider it. But I was wrong about that.

Wasn't till I turned on TV that I started taking the whole thing seriously. I mean, Jimmy Lee tends to exaggerate anyhow, and I figured he's just trying to get me to do what he wanted. But here were Lisa Jensen and Mike Rudd, the newspeople from Channel 13, and they looked scared. Lisa's perfect blonde hair was actually poked out on one side of her head, first time I'd ever seen such a thing. The coast was being evacuated, they said. In the pictures they showed, palm trees were already blowing sideways.

As I gathered candles and a flashlight and filled the guest-room tub with water, the wind gathered itself, too. Seemed to follow me around the house, gusting louder by the minute. I was peering out the upstairs hall window, trying to see could I catch signs of life next door at the Marchants', when the lights went, like blinking your eye and then not being able to get it open again. Pitch black, without even the red and yellow lights you get behind closed eyes. The wind yammered against the window, and I backed off into the blackness of my house.

Northeast corner's the best place to be in a tornado, read that somewhere. Figured it wouldn't hurt in a hurricane either. Trouble is, I didn't know where northeast was. So I settled for our bedroom, which at least was familiar. Sat myself on the bed with a radio and flashlight, to wait out the storm.

Time crept along like a whipped puppy, whimpering and inching its way around the clock face. Five minutes took hours. The howl of the wind became the only truth there was. At first I could hear other sounds—bumps and crashes all around, my mind racing to imagine what each one was—but after while there was nothing but screaming, howling wind, pulse after pulse of it, beating like a powerful, angry heart, so loud I couldn't hear the radio turned full blast and held right by my ear, so loud it took over my body, meshing with that buzzing in my head, making itself part of me. Changing my inside land-scape forever.

Sometime during the night, I left my bedroom, groped down the stairs and ended up on the hall floor—not a corner, but at least windowless. Maybe at some point I dozed off, I can't recall, though it seems unlikely, what with every bone and muscle and nerve in my body standing exposed, ready to face death. And maybe I thought back over my life, how they say you do when you're about to drown. But if so, I've blanked it out now. All I remember is wind.

The world turned light gradual as the wind died. Can't say how it happened, just that I all of a sudden realized I could hear again, and see. Standing was a chore, both legs cramped and stiff. Even flexing my fingers hurt. Seem like I'd been curled up in a ball for years, like Rip Van Winkle waking after his long sleep to find a changed world.

Though changed seems too mild to describe what'd happened overnight.

Walking down the hall, I turned the corner and stood in the doorway to our dining room. It was dark. I could hardly see. Took me a minute to figure why: in place of the big bay window was a treetop, pushing its way about a foot into the room, filling the air with the smell of oak leaves and Spanish moss, a piece of which dangled like mistletoe from my chandelier. The sunlight seeping through the branches set a thousand pieces of broken glass on the dining room table to glittering fire.

Those tiny points danced inside my eyelids as I walked into the kitchen, where it wasn't easy to separate my mess from Dion's. What caught my eye at that point was outside anyhow. Through the back-door window I saw what was left of our garage, roof pried up like the top of a tin can, one side collapsed where the mulberry tree'd crashed into it.

Opened the back door to see better. The sun shone so bright I had to squint against it. Outside, the air was still — not a sound anywhere, neither cricket nor bird, nor even a breeze. Nothing. A soundless bright morning like you might imagine after the world was done, else before it'd begun.

Would've walked on outside then, but thought better of it when I saw my back stoop was gone, whished away by the wind, nowhere in sight. Stepping back and looking down, I saw bloody footprints on my white tile floor, footprints which followed me like red shadows back down the hall, up the stairs and into the hall bath where I rinsed them to discover tiny criss-cross cuts from heel to toe. I hadn't felt a thing, and still did not, as I dried and bandaged them.

While my body moved, my mind floated in its own strange limbo. I only registered that I looked into the bathroom mirror and ran my fingers through my hair, that I went into my bedroom where the worst of it was a broken window which had let in rain and wind, knocking over a porcelain lamp I'd got down at the store at a discount on account of it was chipped. That I put shoes on my bandaged feet, trying not to look out the window anymore than I had to, now; some part of me knowing you had to take this slow. Pace yourself, for protection.

Since the front door wouldn't budge, I had to use the back. Sitting on the floor, I pushed off. My feet hurt when they hit the ground.

Pearl Street was unrecognizable. Invisible, really. Tree over tree over tree, pickup sticks — here uprooted, jagged brown fingers reaching for sky; there snapped in two, raw white innards gleaming in the sun. Ravaged. Devastation. Hadn't eaten since noon the day before, but I bent at the end of where my driveway used to be and gave over the remains of yesterday's tuna sandwich.

Though my brain was in neutral, my feet seemed to have an idea where they were headed. Pure instinct guided them down Pearl to what had been the corner of Hadley, where they took a right. Climbing and clambering over trees, I took note of Steven Haselwood opening his front door, bald spot shining, glasses crooked, mouth gaped wide. Saw Mart Temple looking out through the broken glass of her picture window. You could see clear through her nightgown, on account of how the sun was, which would have embarrassed Miss Mart no end if she'd known, her being a churchgoer and a widow, not to mention eighty-some years old. Her prize-winning flower beds were gone, too. As my feet made their way onto Winslow Ave, I saw Louie Nexsen in his yard — down on his knees, like he's praying. Through it all, the silence and the brightness burned together. And we none of us spoke to the other.

Mizz T's house is smack in the middle of Winslow Ave. Yesterday, it was helpful to know that, though not foolproof, since even locating the middle of a block wasn't a sure bet. It was like a nightmare: you knew where everything should be, but none of it was, else it was in a form so changed as to be past recognizing. Few years ago, I saw a picture of this painting where clocks were melting and another one, where hands stuck out of the unlikeliest places. Yesterday was like that. And your mind plumb goes numb with it.

That's what mine did as I stood at the head of where I reckoned Mizz T's drive was. Of the eight huge oaks used to lead up to the house, wasn't but one left, and it beat all to hell. Couldn't see the house from where I stood.

After I fought my way in that general direction a piece, this idea pushed through my numbness: couldn't see the house from where *anybody* stood. Wasn't there.

I was wrong, though. Some of it was. The second story was gone, and parts of the first. In the ruins of his momma's dining room I found her son, ghost pale and still, standing in the middle of where her walnut dropleaf table'd been, a spot where we'd shared many a silent, unhappy meal. Nothing to show for it now but tree limbs, trash, and whatever memories we'd keep.

"Hey, Mat." His voice had about as much color as his face. All his boyness was gone, and what I saw in its place was the way little old men's faces get, pinched and turned in on themselves.

"Hey, Jimmy Lee." We stood there contemplating the mess like a couple of strangers at a Moose Club get-together. And me remembering all the things Mizz T'd been saving for good, things which would've been mine—ours. Gone now, in a gust of cleansing wind.

"C'mon." I took Jimmy Lee's hand to lead him back the way I'd come, back to our house, which on balance was in pretty good shape. At the top of Mizz T's drive I stopped and looked back, knowing for a fact something I only guessed at the day before: I'd of died in there. One way or the other.

Knowing that helped me do what had to be done. That and the numbness, a sense of putting one foot in front of the other and moving forward, regardless of the cost.

Didn't start talking till we got to the house, where I boiled water on a camp stove and fixed us both coffee. Then I didn't stop for what seemed like hours.

Wonder how I thought he'd take it? I can't say. Because of my being so tired, I figured he was too. I reckoned he'd be relieved, not just after the night before, but after all the years we'd put in together. Whatever we started out as, seem like we'd got to the point where we just tolerated each other on the best days. Others, it was a whole lot worse. And though I thought I hadn't seen my life flash by me the night before, maybe I did after all, because it seemed suddenly clear to me that the two of us're just shadows — of ourselves and maybe even each other — both hungering after wholeness the other can't offer; struggling in a dim light to be, and never connecting in the deepest places, where it counts for something.

What I'd come to sometime during the night was this: we *could* reverse mistakes we'd made on account of Jimmy Lee's being crazy about big bosoms and me saying one unaccountable yes twenty-two years back. We could change the face of our future. Wasn't a thing in this world writ in stone except the end, which this wasn't.

But Jimmy Lee surprised me, how he took it. Set his coffee down, moved to where I sat, knelt on the floor amongst broken crockery, put his arms around my middle and his head in my lap, and held me. At first, he didn't cry or say a word. Looking down on where his hair's thinning out, I felt stiff and uncomfortable, my knees tight together, his chin poking into my thigh. Little by little, he held me tighter, squeezed me to him, while I sat silent above him. Then his shoulders went to shaking and he held me even tighter, crying in a way that hurt my throat till I had to do it too, got down on my knees on the floor beside him and we held each other and cried together, loud and strong, the ruins of our kitchen all about us. Cried till the noise of helicopters and chainsaws split the air and our sorrow sounds were swallowed up in the noise of reclamation.

Those sounds didn't let up till dark last night, and they'll start back at first light, any minute now — follow-up to the roar of Dion, which'll fill our heads for days and weeks to come, I reckon. They'll even drown out that sound of dripping water's driving me crazy, so I won't have to go looking for the source.

Here's the thing: if I look long and hard enough, I could dredge up so many things to be sorry for that it'd take the rest of my life to count them up. Which at this point's time I'm not prepared to spare. Because the wind has blown through, and I'm tired of forever looking back.

Have to keep reminding myself of this: nobody died. Seem like somebody did, but they didn't. It's just that life'll never be the same — so much gone past saving. And me not able yet to see how much of it to mourn.

Epilogue

Circle's getting smaller now. I touch the smooth
brown part around the nipple. Skin there must be the
softest on a woman's body, like velvet, except when it
gets hard and puckery, when you're cold, or excited.

I remember in the early days, how Jimmy Lee'd put
his mouth on my breast and suck like a baby goat. He
could do it for hours, seem like. Looking down at the
top of his head, I was forever torn between wanting
to stroke his hair and murmur something sweet, and
wanting to grab him by the ears, pull his face away
from me, and scream at him to stop, did he think I
was his momma?

Take the nipple lightly between two fingers.

I read it again, and I can't put it off any longer, so
this time I follow Margaret A.'s instructions. I can
almost hear her clear, high voice saying the words out
loud, acting like it's perfectly normal to be going

round in circles looking for the thing that's waiting somewhere, like a bullet for Thomas Joseph Jordan, or a beam for the back of Bobby McAllister's head. Hiding inside, biding its time, like the thick, black slime that rose up to thin Mizz T to bones and thief her breath. Like a rising-up feeling, an angry wind blowing out of the blue, sweeping away the past.

But the past doesn't sweep away that easy. When I left Red Hill after Hurricane Dion, I didn't reckon on coming back. Figured I'd make me a new life somewhere, away from the terrible destruction I'd left behind. But I couldn't leave it. Carried it with me, and a few weeks later it brought me back here, where I want to be after all.

Found me this little place on the outskirts of town, with a yard, and a fence, and a garden, needs tending something awful. Renting for now, but Fred Simmons, a new lawyer in town, is drawing up papers for me to put something down on it. Between my half the insurance money on Mizz T's house and the rest of my legacy, I figure I can make the payments all right.

Garden out back wasn't hurt too bad in the storm, but it's been grown over so many years it'll be a miracle if I can get it going again, which it wouldn't be the first one around here. Right now it's February, and seventy-five degrees outside. Azaleas're so confused they're blooming their fool heads off—pear trees, too. We still don't have any squirrels or possums—trying to find their way back from kingdom come, I reckon. But we've got flowers in places where no flowers ever were before. Liable to find a mess of petunias growing up through cracks in con-crete. Just below the surface, everywhere you look, things're trying to bloom: jonquils, daffodils, nar-cissus. All trying to show their colors.

My friend Ginnie says it's not a miracle. Says it's a well-known fact that hurricanes like Dion send nature into a tailspin, after which something like adrenaline runs through flowers and trees while they try to get their bearings back. That's what's going on now, she says, and I reckon she should know, being a librarian. But I just let it go at a miracle.

Got to finish up now, else be late for my appoint-ment with Fred, who says we still got to wrap up a few details on this contract. Last week when I was in, he asked could we maybe go to the show sometime. Told him I'd have to think about it, and I still hadn't decided, though there is something appealing in the line of his jaw.

When Jimmy Lee called yesterday, wanting to know could we go out to dinner one night next week, I gave him the same answer, which he took with fairly good grace. And isn't it funny how, after so many years of staying up nights to the tune of his snoring, I find it hard sometimes now to sleep without it. Like getting used to hard rain on a tin roof. Not that I'd go back to what we had. Still, I am amazed at how life keeps shifting.

Speaking of which, I called my momma last week and told her what all's happened since I visited. She said the Lord works in mysterious ways. In spite of that I asked her to come visit me sometime, which she said she just might.

I close the book on Margaret A. Swinton now because I'm past pretending this isn't something I can do alone.

And lying here testing these breasts that're more than I ever wanted and less than I ever needed, looking for whatever it is lies below the surface, I grit my teeth, squeeze my nipple, and hold my breath. As I look down, I'm clear on one thing: I'm not so much looking for death when I do this, as life.

SOUTH CAROLINA STATE LIBRARY

0 01 01 015

OCT 30 1992

WITHDRAWN

NO 18 '93

NO 27 '93

MAR 11 1994

NOV 18 1994

JAN 5 1995

JUN 16 1995

JUL 12 1995

Printed
in USA